SPECIAL ANNIVERSARY EDITION

GANGSTA GRANNY

with
EXCLUSIVE
ILLUSTRATIONS
AND ACTIVITIES

This book belongs to

....

David Walliams
GANGSTA GRANNY

Illustrated by Tony Ross

HarperCollins *Children's Books*

First published in hardback in Great Britain by
HarperCollins *Children's Books* 2011
Published in this edition 2018
HarperCollins *Children's Books* is a division of
HarperCollins*Publishers* Ltd,
1 London Bridge Street, London SE1 9GF

www.harpercollins.co.uk

HarperCollins*Publishers*
1st Floor, Watermarque Building, Ringsend Road
Dublin 4, Ireland

113

ISBN 978-0-00737146-4

Printed and bound in the UK using 100% renewable electricity
at CPI Group (UK) Ltd.

For Philip Onyango...

...the bravest little boy I have ever met.

AN INTRODUCTION TO

GANGSTA GRANNY

BY

David Walliams

To my shame, I used to find my granny boring when I was a child. I would dread being sent off to stay the night with her. When I was a boy, Granny had always been old. As far as I was concerned, she'd been born old and wrinkly. Sometimes I would see black-and-white pictures of a young lady who looked like her in frames around her flat, but I couldn't reconcile this person with the one I knew. It seemed impossible that they were one and the same.

My grandma was much like the granny in this book. Her home smelled inexplicably of cabbage, whether she'd cooked cabbage or not.

She kept a used handkerchief tucked up her sleeve at all times. Scrabble was her favourite game. Bottom burps would escape when she crossed the room, sounding exactly like a duck quacking.

One day I asked Granny about World War II. I'd been learning about it at school in History lessons. Suddenly this old lady became animated in a way I'd never seen before. Her eyes lit up. Her words tumbled out. For what seemed like hours, she told me of her adventures from forty years before. As Nazi bombs rained down on London during the Blitz, she'd had to hide in the Underground train tunnels.

"We would hear the air-raid sirens and rush down the steps. Women and children first. There would be hundreds of us huddled down there, lying next to each other, sleeping on the cold floor under our coats as we heard the explosions up above. When we came up in the morning, we wouldn't know if our houses would still be standing. Once a double-decker bus was blown apart on my street. So many souls lost."

Needless to say, she had me entranced. I realised then that my grandma had lived through infinitely more thrilling times than I ever had, or ever would.

When this conversation happened, I was the same age as Ben in this book, probably eleven or twelve. At that time, becoming a children's author was not my ambition. I wanted to be James Bond, Sherlock Holmes or Tarzan. I still do! So I was not thinking that this conversation could be the beginning of a story.

However, nearly thirty years later, I began writing my fourth children's novel. My grandmother had died a decade before, and I wanted to honour her memory somehow. I felt I had an important message for my young readers – that, just because someone is old, it doesn't mean they are boring. If you are lucky enough to have grandparents, all you have to do is take the time to ask them about their lives.

At book signings I always have lots of women of a certain age tell me that they are a real-life "gangsta granny". This always makes me happy.

Of course, my grandmother was not an international jewel thief! That is where my imagination took over. I wanted Ben and Granny to take on the biggest heist in history. Ian Fleming had got there first with Fort Knox in the James Bond classic Goldfinger. *The Crown Jewels seemed like the perfect choice. They are iconic, priceless and, of course, British.*

When I first planned the story, I had no idea that Her Majesty the Queen would make an appearance. To be honest, I'd become stuck at a certain point in the book. I was trying to think who would be the worst person to bump into if you were in the Tower of London trying to steal the Crown Jewels. The answer was, as always, a simple one: their owner!

I've been fortunate enough to meet the real Queen on a handful of occasions. However, one of the things you're told not to do when you speak to her is ask her a question. As you can imagine, this makes conversation hard. So I've never been able to enquire, "Do you know you are a character in my story?" I would love to know. If I were her, I'd be intrigued, and maybe *even demand an appearance fee!*

If I'm lucky enough to live a long life and become a grandparent, I hope my grandchildren won't assume I'm boring just because I am old. Because, of course, everyone has a story to tell. All you have to do is ask.

David Walliams

1

CABBAGY WATER

"But Granny is soooo boring," said Ben. It was a cold Friday evening in November, and as usual he was slumped in the back of his mum and dad's car. Once again he was on his way to stay the night at his dreaded granny's house. "*All* old people are."

"Don't talk about your granny like that," said Dad weakly, his fat stomach pushed up against the steering wheel of the family's little brown car.

"I hate spending time with her," protested Ben. "Her TV doesn't work, all she wants to do is play SCRABBLE and she stinks of cabbage!"

"In fairness to the boy she does stink of **cabbage**," agreed Mum, as she applied some last minute lip-liner.

"You're not helping, wife," muttered Dad. "At worst my mother has a very slight odour of boiled vegetables."

"Can't I come with you?" pleaded Ben. "I love ball-whatsit dancing," he lied.

"It's called **ballroom dancing**," corrected Dad. "And you don't love it. You said, and I quote, 'I would rather eat my own bogeys than watch that rubbish'."

Now, Ben's mum and dad *loved* **ballroom dancing.** Sometimes Ben thought they loved it more than they loved him. There was a TV show on Saturday evenings that Mum and Dad never missed called **STRICTLY STARS DANCING**, where celebrities would be paired with professional ballroom dancers.

In fact, if there was a fire in their house, and Mum could only save either a sparkly gold tap-shoe once worn by **Flavio Flavioli** (the shiny, tanned dancer and heartbreaker from Italy who appeared on every series of the hit TV show) or her only child, Ben thought she would probably go for the shoe. Tonight, his mum and dad were going to an arena to see **STRICTLY STARS DANCING** live on stage.

"I don't know why you don't give up on this pipe dream of becoming a plumber, Ben, and think about dancing professionally," said Mum, her lip-liner scrawling across her cheek as the car bounced over a particularly bumpy speed bump. Mum had a habit of applying make-up in the car, which meant she often arrived somewhere looking like a clown. "Maybe, just maybe, you could end up on **STRICTLY!**" added Mum excitedly.

"Because prancing around like that is stupid," said Ben.

Mum whimpered a little, and reached for a tissue.

"You're upsetting your mother. Now just be quiet, please, Ben, there's a good boy," replied Dad firmly, as he turned up the volume on the stereo. Inevitably, a **STRICTLY** CD was playing. *50 Golden Greats from the Hit TV Show* was emblazoned on the cover. Ben hated the CD, not least because he had heard it a million times. In fact, he had heard it so many times it was like torture.

Ben's mum worked at the local nail salon, **GAIL'S NAILS**. Because there weren't many customers, Mum and the other lady who worked there (unsurprisingly called Gail) spent most days doing each other's nails. Buffing, cleaning, trimming, moisturising, coating, sealing, polishing, filing, lacquering, extending and painting. They were doing things to each other's nails all day long (unless **Flavio Flavioli** was on daytime TV). That meant Mum would always come home with extremely long multi-coloured plastic extensions on the end of her fingers.

Ben's dad, meanwhile, worked as a security guard at the local supermarket. The highlight of his twenty-year career thus far was stopping an old man who had concealed two tubs of margarine down his trousers. Although Dad was now too fat to run after any robbers, he could certainly block their escape. Dad met Mum when he wrongly accused her of shoplifting a bag of crisps, and within a year they were married.

The car swung round the corner into **GREY CLOSE,** where Granny's bungalow squatted. It was one of a whole row of sad little homes, mainly inhabited by old people.

The car came to a halt, and Ben slowly turned his head towards the bungalow. Looking expectantly out of the living-room window was Granny. Waiting. Waiting. She was always waiting by the window for him to arrive. *How long has she been there?* thought Ben. *Since last week?*

Ben was her only grandchild and, as far as he knew, no one else ever came to visit.

Granny waved and gave Ben a little smile, which his grumpy face just about permitted him to reluctantly return.

"Right, one of us will pick you up tomorrow morning at around eleven," said Dad, keeping the engine running.

"Can't you make it ten?"

"Ben!" growled Dad. He released the child lock and Ben grudgingly pushed the door open and stepped out. Ben didn't need the child lock, of course: he was eleven years old and hardly likely to open the door while the car was driving. He suspected his dad only used it to stop him from diving out of the car when they were on their way to Granny's house. **CLUNK** went the door behind him, as the engine revved up again.

Before he could ring the bell, Granny opened the door. A huge gust of **cabbage** blasted in Ben's face. It was like a great big slap of smell.

She was very much your textbook granny:

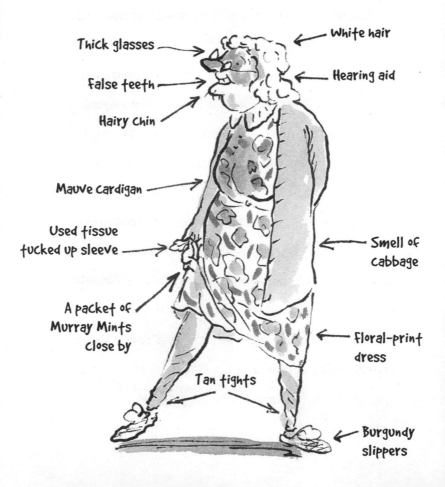

Thick glasses

White hair

False teeth

Hearing aid

Hairy chin

Mauve cardigan

Used tissue tucked up sleeve

Smell of cabbage

A packet of Murray Mints close by

Floral-print dress

Tan tights

Burgundy slippers

"Are Mummy and Daddy not coming in?" she asked, a little crestfallen. This was one of the things Ben couldn't stand about her: she was always talking to him like he was a baby.

Broom-broom-brroooooooooommm.

Together Granny and Ben watched the little brown car race off, leaping over the speed bumps. Mum and Dad didn't like spending time with her any more than Ben did. It was just a convenient place to dump him on a Friday night.

"No, erm… Sorry, Granny…" spluttered Ben.

"Oh, well, come in then," she muttered. "Now, I've set up the SCRABBLE board and for your tea, I've got your favourite… cabbage soup!"

Ben's face dropped even further. *Nooooooooo ooooooooo!* he thought.

2

A DUCK QUACKING

Before long, granny and grandson were sitting opposite each other in deadly silence at the dining-room table. Just like every single Friday night.

When his parents weren't watching **STRICTLY** on TV, they were eating curry or going to the movies. Friday night was their "date night", and ever since Ben could remember, they had been dropping him off with his granny when they went out. If they weren't going to see **STRICTLY STARS DANCING LIVE ON STAGE LIVE!**, they would normally go to the

Taj Mahal (the curry house on the high street, not the ancient white marble monument in India) and eat their own bodyweight in poppadoms.

All that could be heard in the bungalow was the TICKING of the carriage clock on the mantelpiece, the clinking of metal spoons against porcelain bowls, and the occasional high-pitched whistle of Granny's faulty hearing aid. It was a device whose purpose seemed to be not so much to aid Granny's deafness, but to cause deafness in others.

It was one of the main things that Ben hated about his granny. The others were:

1) Granny would always spit in the used tissue she kept up the sleeve of her cardigan and wipe her grandson's face with it.

2) Her TV had been broken since 1992. And now it was covered in dust so thick it was like fur.

3) Her house was **stuffed** full of books and she was always trying to get Ben to read them even though he loathed reading.

4) Granny insisted you wore a heavy winter coat all year round even on a boiling hot day, otherwise you wouldn't "feel the benefit".

5) She reeked of cabbage. (Anyone with a cabbage allergy would not be able to come within ten miles of her.)

6) Granny's idea of an exciting day out was feeding mouldy crusts of bread to some ducks in a pond.

7) She constantly blew off without even acknowledging it.

8) Those blow-offs didn't just smell of **cabbage**. They smelled of rotten **cabbage**.

9) Granny made you go to bed so early it seemed hardly worthwhile getting up in the first place.

10) She knitted her only grandson jumpers for Christmas with puppies or kittens on them, which he was forced to wear during the whole festive period by his parents.

"How's your soup?" enquired the old lady.

Ben had been stirring the pale green liquid around the chipped bowl for the last ten minutes hoping it would somehow disappear.

It wouldn't.

And now it was getting cold.

Cold bits of **cabbage**, floating around in some cold **cabbagy** water.

"Erm, it's delicious, thank you," replied Ben.

"Good."

TICK TOCK TICK TOCK.

"Good," said the old lady again.

Clink. Clink.

"Good." Granny seemed to find it as hard to speak to Ben as he did to her.

Clink clank. Whistle.

"How's school?" she asked.

"Boring," muttered Ben. Adults always ask kids how they are doing at school. The one subject kids absolutely hate talking about. You don't even want to talk about school when you are *at* school.

"Oh," said Granny.

TICK TOCK **clink clank** whistle TICK TOCK.

"Well, I must check on the oven," said Granny after the long pause stretched out into an even longer pause. "I've got your favourite cabbage pie on the go."

She rose slowly from her seat and made her

way to the kitchen. As she took each step a little bubble of wind puffed out of her saggy bottom. It sounded like a duck quacking. Either she didn't realise or was extremely good at pretending she didn't realise.

Ben watched her go, and then c r e p t silently across the room. This was difficult because of the piles of books everywhere. Ben's granny LOVED books, and always seemed to have her nose in one. They were stacked on shelves, lined up on windowsills, piled up in corners.

Crime novels were her favourite. Books about gangstas, bank robbers, the mafia and the like. Ben wasn't sure what the difference between a gangsta and a gangster was, but a gangsta seemed much worse.

Although Ben hated reading, he loved looking at all the covers of Granny's books. They had fast cars and guns and glamorous ladies luridly painted on them, and Ben found it hard to believe this boring old granny of his liked reading stories that looked so thrilling.

Why is she obsessed with gangstas? thought Ben. *Gangstas don't live in bungalows. Gangstas don't play* SCRABBLE. *Gangstas probably don't smell of* cabbage.

Ben was a very slow reader, and the teachers at school made him feel stupid because he couldn't keep up. The headmistress had even put him down a year in the hope that he would catch up on his reading. As a result, all his friends were in a different class, and he felt nearly as lonely at school as he did at home, with his parents who only cared about **ballroom dancing.**

Eventually, after a hairy moment where he nearly knocked over a stack of real-life crime books, Ben made it to the pot plant in the corner.

He quickly tipped the remainder of his soup

into it. The plant looked as if it was already dying, and if it wasn't dead yet, Granny's cold cabbage soup was sure to kill it off.

Suddenly, Ben heard Granny's bum squeaking again as she made her way into the dining room, so he sped back to the table. He sat there trying to look as innocent as possible, with his empty bowl in front of him and his spoon in his hand.

"I've finished my soup, thank you, Granny. It was yummy!"

"That's good," said the old lady as she trundled back to the table carrying a saucepan on a tray. "I've got plenty more here for you, boy!" Smiling, she served him up another bowl.

Ben gulped in terror.

3

"I can't find **PLUMBING WEEKLY**, Raj," said Ben.

It was the next Friday, and the boy had been scouring the magazine shelves of the local newsagent's shop. He couldn't find his favourite publication anywhere. The magazine was aimed at professional plumbers, and Ben was beguiled by pages and pages of pipes, taps, cisterns, ballcocks, boilers, tanks and drains. **PLUMBING WEEKLY** was the only thing he enjoyed reading – mainly because it was crammed full of pictures and diagrams.

Ever since he had been old enough to hold

33

things, Ben had *loved* plumbing. When other children were playing with ducks in the bath, Ben had asked his parents for bits of pipe, and made complicated water channelling systems. If a tap broke in the house, he fixed it. If a toilet was blocked, Ben wasn't disgusted, he was ecstatic!

Ben's parents didn't approve of him wanting to be a plumber, though. They wanted him to be **rich** and **famous,** and to their knowledge there had never been a **rich** and **famous** plumber. Ben was as good with his hands as he was rubbish at reading, and was absolutely fascinated when a plumber came round to fix a leak. He would watch in awe, as a junior doctor might watch a great surgeon at work in an operating theatre.

But he always felt like a disappointment to his mum and dad. They desperately wanted him to fulfil the ambition they had never managed:

to become a professional ballroom dancer. Ben's mum and dad had discovered their love of **ballroom dancing** too late to become champions themselves. And, to be honest, they seemed to prefer sitting on their bums watching it on TV to actually taking part.

As such, Ben tried to keep his passion private. To avoid hurting his mum and dad's feelings, he stashed his copies of **PLUMBING WEEKLY** under his bed. And he had made an arrangement with Raj, so that every week the newsagent would keep the plumbing magazine aside for him. Now, though, he couldn't find it anywhere.

Ben had searched for the magazine behind *Kerrang!* and *Heat* and even looked underneath *The Lady* (not an actual lady, I mean the magazine called *The Lady*), all to no avail. Raj's store was madly messy, but people came from miles away to shop there as he always brought a smile to their faces.

Raj was halfway up a stepladder, putting up Christmas decorations. Well, I say "Christmas decorations" – he was actually putting up a banner that read "Happy Birthday", though he had Tippexed out the word "Birthday" and replaced it in scratchy biro with "Christmas".

Raj carefully stepped down off the ladder to help Ben with his search.

"Your **PLUMBING WEEKLY**... mmm... Let me think, have you looked beside the toffee bonbons?" said Raj.

"Yes," replied Ben.

"And it's not underneath the colouring books?"

"No."

"And you have checked behind the penny chews?"

"Yes."

"Well, this is very mysterious. I know I ordered one in for you, young Ben. Mmm, very mysterious..." Raj was speaking extremely slowly, in that way people do when they are thinking. "I am so sorry, Ben, I know you love it, but I don't have a clue where it is. I do have a special offer on Cornettos."

"It's November, Raj, it's **FREEZING** outside!" said Ben. "Who would want to eat a Cornetto now?"

"Everyone when they hear my special offer! Wait until you hear this: buy twenty-three Cornettos, get one free!"

"Why on earth would I want twenty-four Cornettos?!" said Ben with a laugh.

"Erm, well, I don't know, you could maybe eat twelve, and put the other twelve in your pocket to enjoy later."

"That's a lot of Cornettos, Raj. Why are you

so keen to get rid of them?"

"They go out of date tomorrow," said Raj, as he lumbered over to the freezer cabinet, slid open the glass top and pulled out a cardboard box of Cornettos. A **FREEZING**-cold mist immediately

shrouded the shop. "Look! Best Before 15th of November."

Ben studied the box. "It says Best Before 15th of November 1996."

"Well," said Raj. "Even more reason to put them on special offer. OK, Ben, this is my final offer. Buy one box of Cornettos, I will give you ten boxes absolutely free!"

"Really, Raj, no thanks," said Ben. He peered into the freezer cabinet to see what else might be **lurking** in there. It had never been defrosted and Ben wouldn't have been surprised to find a perfectly preserved woolly mammoth from the Ice Age inside.

"Hang on," he said, as he moved a few frost-encrusted ice lollies out of the way. "It's in here! **PLUMBING WEEKLY!**"

"Ah yes, I remember now," said Raj. "I put it in there to keep it fresh for you."

"Fresh?" said Ben.

"Well, young man, the magazine comes out on a Tuesday, but it's Friday today. So I put it in the freezer to keep it fresh for you, Ben. I didn't want it to go off."

Ben wasn't sure how any magazine could ever go off, but he thanked the newsagent anyway. "That's very kind of you, Raj. And I'll have a packet of Rolos, please."

"I can offer you seventy-three packets of Rolos for the price of seventy-two!" exclaimed the newsagent with a smile that was meant to entice.

"No thanks, Raj."

"One thousand packets of Rolos for the price of nine hundred and ninety-eight?"

"No thanks," said Ben.

"Are you mad, Ben? That's a wonderful offer. All right, all right, you drive a hard bargain, Ben.

One million and seven packets of Rolos, for the price of a million and four. That's three packets of Rolos absolutely free!"

"I'll just take one packet and the magazine, thank you."

"Of course, young sir!"

"I can't wait to get stuck into **PLUMBING WEEKLY** later. I have to go and spend the whole night with my boring old granny again."

It had been a week since Ben's last visit, and the dreaded Friday had rolled around once more. His parents were going to see a `"chick flick"`, according to his mum. Romance and kissing and all that goo. Yuckety yuck yuck.

"Tut tut tut," said Raj, shaking his head as he counted out Ben's change.

Ben instantly felt ashamed. He had never seen the newsagent do this before. Like all the other local kids, Ben regarded Raj as "one of us" not "one of them". He was so full of life and laughter, Raj seemed a world away from parents and teachers and all the grown-ups who felt they could tell you off because they were bigger than you.

"Just because your granny is old, young Ben," said Raj, "doesn't mean that she is boring. I am getting on a bit myself. And whenever I have met your granny I have found her to be a very interesting lady."

"But—"

"Don't be too hard on her, Ben," pleaded Raj. "We will all be old one day. Even you. And I'm sure your granny will have a secret or two. Old people always do…"

4

Ben wasn't at all sure that Raj was right about Granny. That night it was the same old story. Granny served up cabbage soup, followed by cabbage pie and for dessert it was cabbage mousse. She even found some cabbage-flavoured after-dinner chocolates* somewhere. After dinner, Granny and Ben sat down together on the musty sofa as they always did.

"SCRABBLE time!" exclaimed Granny.

---

* Cabbage-flavoured chocolates are not as nice as they sound, and they don't sound that nice.

Great, thought Ben. *Tonight's going to be a million times more boring than last week!*

Ben detested SCRABBLE. If he had his way, Ben would build a rocket, and **blast** all the SCRABBLE boards in the world into outer space. Granny pulled out the dusty old SCRABBLE box from the sideboard and set up the game on the pouffe.

Ben sighed.

What seemed like decades later, but was probably just hours, Ben stared at his letters, before scanning the board. He had already put down:

BORING

ANCIENT

QUACK (double-word score)

POINTLESS

PONGY (this had to be checked in the dictionary)

WRINKLES

CABBAGESICK (triple-word score)

ESCAPE

HELP

IHATETHISSTUPIDGAME (Granny had disallowed this on account of it not being one word.)

He had an "E", an "M", an "I", a "U" and a "D". Granny had just put down "MURRAYMINT" (double-word score) so Ben used the "T" at the end to form the word "TEDIUM".

"Well, it's nearly eight o'clock, young man," announced Granny, looking at her little gold watch. "Time for your beddy-byes, I think…"

Ben groaned inwardly. Beddy-byes! He wasn't a toddler!

"But I don't have to go to bed until nine o'clock at home!" he protested. "And not until ten o'clock when I haven't got school in the morning."

"No, Ben, off you go to bed, please." The old lady could be quite firm when she wanted to be. "And don't forget to brush your teeth. I'll be up soon to give you a bedtime story, if you like. You always used to love a bedtime story."

Later, Ben stood at the sink in the bathroom. It was a cold, damp room with no window. Some of the tiles had fallen off the wall. There was just one sad little frayed towel and a very worn bar of soap that looked like it was half soap, half mould.

Ben **hated** brushing his teeth. So he pretended to brush his teeth. Pretending to brush your teeth is simple. Don't tell your parents I told you, but if you want to try it for yourself, all you have to do is follow this handy step-by-step guide:

1) Turn on the cold tap

2) Wet the toothbrush

3) Squeeze a tiny amount of toothpaste on to your finger and place finger in mouth

4) Move the trace of toothpaste around your mouth with your tongue

5) Spit

6) Turn off the tap

See? It's so easy. Nearly as easy as brushing your teeth.

Ben looked at himself in the bathroom mirror. He was eleven years old, but shorter than he wanted to be, so he stood on his tiptoes for a moment. Ben was aching to be older.

Only a few more years, he thought, and he would be taller and hairier and **spottier,** and his Friday nights would be very different.

He wouldn't have to stay at boring old Granny's any more. Instead Ben would be able to do all the thrilling things the older kids in the town did on Friday nights:

Hang around with a gang of friends outside the off-licence waiting for someone to tell you off.

Or alternatively, sit at the bus stop with some girls in tracksuits and chew gum and never actually get on a bus.

Yes, a world of mystery and Wonder awaited him.

However, for now, even though it was still light outside and he could hear boys in the nearby park playing football, it was time for Ben to go to sleep. In a hard little bed in a damp little room in his granny's rundown little bungalow. That smelled of cabbage.

Not just a little bit.

A lot.

Sighing, Ben got under the covers.

Just then, Granny gently opened the door to his bedroom. He quickly shut his eyes and pretended to be asleep. She lumbered over to the bed, and Ben could feel her standing over him for a moment.

"I was going to tell you that bedtime story," she whispered. The old lady had often told him stories when he was younger, about pirates and smugglers and master criminals, but he was far too old for all that nonsense now.

"What a shame you're asleep already," she said. "Well, I just wanted to say that I love you. Goodnight, my little Benny."

He hated being called "Benny" too.

And "little".

The nightmare continued, as Ben sensed his granny bending over to give him a kiss. The prickly old hairs on her chin bristled uncomfortably against his cheek. Then he heard the familiar rhythmic quacking sound as her bum squeaked with every step. She squeaked her way back to the door and closed it behind her, sealing the smell in.

That's it, thought Ben. I have to escape!

5

A LITTLE BROKEN

"Aaaahhhhkkkk…pffftttt…aaaaaahhhhhk kkkkk … pppppppfffffffffffffttttttt…"

No, reader, you haven't bought the Swahili edition of this book by mistake. That was the sound Ben was waiting for.

Granny snoring.

She was asleep.

"Aaaaaahhhhkkkkkkk… pppppfffffffffttttttt… aaaaaaaaaaaaahhhhhhkkkkkkk…"

Ben crept out of his room and made his way over to the telephone in the hall. It was one of those old-style telephones that purred like a cat when you dialled a number.

"Mum…?" he whispered.

"I CAN HARDLY HEAR YOU!" she shouted back. There was loud jazz music playing in the background. Mum and Dad were at the arena again watching STRICTLY STARS DANCING LIVE ON STAGE LIVE! She was probably drooling as Flavio Flavioli swivelled his hips and broke the hearts of thousands of women of a certain age. "What's the matter? Is everything all right? The old bat hasn't died, has she?"

"No, she's fine, but I hate it here. Can't you come and pick me up? Please," whispered Ben.

"Flavio hasn't even done his second dance yet."

"Please," he pleaded. "I want to come home. Granny is such a bore. It's torture spending time with her."

"Speak to your dad." Ben heard a muffled sound as she passed the phone over.

"HELLO?" shouted Dad.

"Please keep your voice down!"

"WHAT?" he shouted again.

"Shhhh. Keep your voice down. You are going to wake up Granny. Can you come and pick me up, Dad? Please? I hate it here."

"No, we cannot. Seeing this show is a once-in-a-lifetime experience."

"You saw it last Friday!" protested Ben.

"Twice in a lifetime, then."

"And you said you were going again next Friday too!"

"Look, if I have any more of your cheek, young lad, you can stay with her until Christmas. Goodbye!"

With that, his dad hung up. Ben carefully placed the receiver back in its cradle, and the phone made the quietest TING.

Suddenly, he noticed that Granny's snoring had stopped.

Had she heard what he'd said? He looked behind him and thought he saw her shadow, but then it was gone.

It was true that Ben found her dreadfully dull, but he didn't want her to know that. After all, she was a lonely old widow, and her husband had died long before Ben was even born. Guiltily, Ben crept back to the spare room and waited and waited and waited for the morning.

At breakfast Granny seemed different.

Quieter. Older maybe. A little broken.

Her eyes looked bloodshot as if she'd been crying.

Did she hear? thought Ben. *I really hope she didn't hear.*

She stood by the oven as Ben sat at the tiny kitchen table. Granny was pretending to be interested in her calendar, which was pinned to the wall by the oven. Ben could tell she was pretending, because there was nothing interesting on her calendar.

This was a typical week in Granny's hectic life:

Monday: Make cabbage soup. Play SCRABBLE against myself. Read a book.

Tuesday: Make cabbage pie. Read another book. Blow off.

Wednesday: Make the dish "Chocolate Surprise". The surprise is that it isn't made of chocolate at all. It is in fact one hundred per cent cabbage.

Thursday: Suck a **Murray Mint** all day. (She could make one mint last a lifetime.)

Friday: Still suck the same **Murray Mint.** My wonderful grandson visits.

Saturday: My wonderful grandson leaves. Have another nice sit-down. Pooped!

Sunday: Eat roast cabbage, with braised cabbage and boiled cabbage on the side. Blow off all day.

Eventually, Granny turned away from the calendar. "Your mummy and daddy will be here soon," she finally said, breaking the silence.

"Yes," said Ben, looking at his watch. "Just a few more minutes."

The minutes felt like hours. Days even. Months!

A minute can be a long time. Don't believe me? Then sit in a room on your own and do nothing but count for sixty seconds.

Have you done it yet? I don't believe you. I'm not joking. I want you to really go and do it.

I am not carrying on with the story until you do.

It's not my time I'm wasting.

I've got all day.

Right, have you done it now? Good. Now back to the story...

At just after eleven o'clock, the little brown car pulled up in front of Granny's house. Much like a getaway driver for a bank robbery, Mum kept the engine running. She leaned over and opened the passenger door so Ben could dive in quickly and they could *zoom off.*

As Ben trudged towards the car, Granny stood at the front door. "Would you like to come in for a cup of tea, Linda?" she shouted.

"No thanks," said Ben's mum. "Quick, Ben, for goodness' sake get in!" She **REVVED** the engine. "I don't want to have to talk to the old dear."

"Shh!" said Ben. "She'll hear you!"

"I thought you didn't like Granny?" said Mum.

"I didn't say that, Mum. I said I found her boring. But I don't want *her* to know that, do I?"

Mum laughed as they sped off out of **GREY CLOSE**. "I wouldn't worry, Ben, your granny

isn't really with it. She probably doesn't understand what you're saying half the time."

Ben frowned. He wasn't sure about that. He wasn't sure at all. He remembered Granny's face at the breakfast table. Suddenly, he had a horrible feeling she understood a lot more than he had ever realised…

6

COLD, WET EGG

This Friday night would have been just as spectacularly dull as the last, if Ben hadn't remembered to bring his magazine with him this time. Once again, Mum and Dad dumped their only child at Granny's.

As soon as he arrived, Ben rushed past her into his cold, damp little bedroom, shut the door and read his copy of the latest **PLUMBING WEEKLY** from cover to cover. There was an amazing guide, with lots and lots of colour photographs, showing how to install the new generation of combi boilers. Ben folded over the corner of the page. Now he knew what he wanted for Christmas.

Once he'd finished the magazine, Ben sighed and headed to the living room. He knew he couldn't stay in his bedroom all evening.

Granny looked up and smiled when she saw him. "SCRABBLE time!" she exclaimed cheerily, holding up the board.

The next morning the air was thick with silence.

"Another boiled egg?" said Granny, as they sat in her rundown little kitchen.

Ben didn't like boiled eggs and hadn't finished his first one yet. Granny could even ruin food this simple. The egg would always come out all watery, and the soldiers were always burnt to a cinder. When the old lady wasn't looking, Ben would flick the egg gloop out of the window with his spoon, and hide the soldiers behind the radiator. There must be a whole platoon of them back there by now.

"No thanks, Granny. I'm completely full," replied Ben. "Delicious boiled egg, thank you," he added.

"Mmm…" murmured the old lady, unconvinced. "It's a bit nippy. I'm just going to put another cardigan on," she said, even though she was already wearing two. Granny trundled out of the room, quacking as she went.

Ben flicked the rest of his egg out of the window, and then tried to find something else to eat. He knew that Granny had a secret stash of chocolate biscuits that she kept on a top shelf in the kitchen. Granny would give Ben one on his birthday. Ben would also help himself to one from time to time, when his granny's **cabbage-based** delicacies left him as hungry as a wolf.

So he quickly slid his chair over to the

cupboard and stood on it to reach the biscuits. He lifted the biscuit tin. It was a big Silver Jubilee assortment tin from 1977 that featured a scratched and faded portrait of a much younger Queen Elizabeth II on the lid. It felt really heavy. Much heavier than usual.

Strange.

Ben shook the tin a little. It didn't feel or sound like it had biscuits inside. It was like it had stones or marbles in it.

Even stranger.

Ben unscrewed the lid.

He stared.

And then he stared some more.

He couldn't believe what was inside.

Diamonds! Rings, bracelets, necklaces, earrings, all with great big sparkling diamonds. Diamonds, diamonds and more diamonds!

Ben was no expert, but he thought there must

be thousands of pounds' worth of jewellery in the biscuit tin, maybe even **millions.**

Suddenly, he heard Granny quacking her way into the room. Fumbling desperately, he put the lid back on and placed the tin on the shelf. He leaped down, yanked his chair over and sat at the table.

Glancing at the window, he realised that his flicked egg hadn't flown out into the garden, but was smeared across the glass. Granny would need a blowtorch to get that off if it dried.

So he rushed over to the window and sucked the cold, wet

egg off the glass, then returned to his seat. It was too unpleasant to swallow so, in a panic, Ben kept it in his mouth.

Granny shuffled back into the kitchen wearing her third cardigan.

Still quacking.

"Better get your coat on, young man. Your mummy and daddy will be here in just a tick," she said with a smile.

Ben reluctantly swallowed the cold, wet egg. It slipped down his throat. Yuck, yuck and triple yuck. "Yes," he said, fearing he would vomit and deposit the egg back on the window.

Scrambled.

7

BAGS
OF
MANURE

"Can I stay at Granny's again tonight?" announced Ben from the back seat of his mum and dad's little brown car. The diamonds in the biscuit tin were so puzzling; he was desperate to do some detective work. Maybe even search every nook and cranny of the old lady's bungalow. This was all awfully mysterious. Raj had said his granny might have a secret or two. And it seemed like the newsagent was right! And whatever Granny's secret was, it must be pretty amazing to explain all those diamonds. What if she used to be a zillionaire? Or worked in a **diamond mine?** Or been left them by a *princess?* Ben couldn't wait to find out.

"What?" asked Dad, astonished.

"But you said she was boring," said Mum, equally astonished, irritated even. "You said all old people are."

"I was just joking," said Ben.

Dad studied his son in the rear-view mirror. He found understanding his plumbing-obsessed son hard enough at the best of times. Right now Ben wasn't making any sense at all. "Mmm, well… if you are sure, Ben…"

"I am sure, Dad."

"I'll call her when we get home. Just to check she's not going out."

"Going out!" scoffed Mum. "The old dear hasn't gone out for twenty years!" she added with a chuckle.

Ben wasn't sure why this was funny.

"I took her out to the garden centre that time," protested Dad.

"It was only because you needed someone to help you carry a load of bags of manure," said Mum.

"She had a super day out, though," said Dad, sounding miffed.

Later, Ben sat alone on his bed. His mind was racing.

Where on earth had Granny got the diamonds?

How much were they worth?

Why would she live in that sad little bungalow if she was so rich?

Ben searched and searched his mind, but couldn't find any answers.

Then Dad entered the room.

"Granny's busy. She says she'd love to see you, but she's going out tonight," he announced.

"What?!" spluttered Ben. Granny hardly ever went out – Ben had seen her calendar. The mystery was getting even more mysterious...

8

Ben hid in the bushes outside Granny's bungalow. While Mum and Dad were downstairs in the living room watching **STRICTLY STARS DANCING** on the TV, Ben had slid down the drainpipe outside his bedroom window, and cycled the five miles to Granny's.

This alone was a sign of how curious Ben had become about his granny. He didn't like cycling. His parents were always encouraging him to get more exercise. They told him that being fit was absolutely necessary if you wanted to be a professional dancer. But since it didn't make much difference when you were lying under a sink, screwing in a new length of copper piping, Ben had never willingly taken any exercise.

Until now.

If Granny was really going out for the first time in twenty years, Ben had to know where. It might just hold the key to how she came to have a ton of diamonds in her biscuit tin.

So he huffed and puffed along the canal towpath on his clunky old bike, until he came to GREY CLOSE. The only good thing was that, being November, instead of being drenched in sweat, Ben was only mildly moist.

He had pedalled fast because he knew he didn't have that much time. STRICTLY STARS DANCING seemed to go on for hours, days even, but it had taken Ben half an hour to cycle over to Granny's, and as soon as the show was over Mum would be calling him downstairs for his tea. Ben's parents loved all the TV dancing shows – *Dancing on Ice Skates, So You Think You Might Be Able To Dance A Bit?* – but they were completely obsessed with **STRICTLY STARS DANCING.** They had recorded every single episode, and had an unrivalled collection of *Strictly* memorabilia in the house, including:

- A lime green thong once worn by **Flavio Flavioli,** framed with a photograph of him wearing it

- A **STRICTLY STARS DANCING** real fake leather bookmark

- Some athlete's foot powder signed by **Flavio's** professional dance partner, the Austrian beauty, Eva Bunz

- His and Hers official **STRICTLY STARS DANCING** leg warmers

- A CD of songs nearly used on the show

- A small wig in a jar that had been worn by the presenter, Sir Dirk Doddery

- A life-size cardboard cut-out of **Flavio Flavioli** that had some of Mum's lipstick smudged around the mouth

- Some earwax in a jar that belonged to a celebrity contestant, the politician Dame Rachel Prejudice MP

- A pair of tan tights that smelled of Eva Bunz

- A doodle on a napkin of a man's bottom drawn by the nasty judge,

Craig Malteser-Woodward

- A set of official **STRICTLY STARS DANCING** eggcups
- A half-full tube of Raljex used by **Flavio Flavioli**
- A Craig Malteser-Woodward poseable action figure
- A Hawaiian Hot pizza crust that had been left by **Flavio** (complete with a signed letter of authenticity from Eva Bunz)

It was a Saturday, so after the show had finished the family were going to be having Cheesy Beans and Sausage. Neither Mum nor Dad could cook, but of all the ready-made meals Ben's mum took out of the freezer, pricked with a fork and placed in the microwave for three minutes, this was his favourite. Ben was hungry and didn't want to miss it – which meant he needed to get back from Granny's house quickly. If it had been a Monday night, say, and they were having **Chicken Tikka Lasagne,** or a Wednesday and **Doner Kebab Pizza,** or a Sunday and **Yorkshire Pudding Chow Mein*** was on the menu, Ben wouldn't have been so bothered.

Night was falling. As it was late November it was rapidly growing colder and darker, and Ben was shivering in the bushes as he spied on his granny. *Where can she be going?* thought Ben. *She hardly ever goes out.*

* The supermarket chain where Ben's dad worked liked to bring the cuisine of two countries together in one easily microwaveable pack. By combining dishes from different countries, perhaps they would be able to bring peace to a deeply divided world. Or maybe not.

He saw a shadow move in her bungalow. Then her face appeared at the window, and Ben quickly shot out of view. The bushes rustled. *Shhh!* thought Ben. Had the old lady seen him?

After a few moments the front door opened slowly, and out stepped a figure dressed entirely in black. A black jumper, black leggings, black gloves, black socks, probably even a black bra and knickers. A black balaclava disguised the face, but from the stoop Ben knew it was Granny. She looked like someone from one of the covers of the books she loved reading. She straddled her mobility scooter and revved the engine.

Where on earth was she going?

And, more importantly, why was she dressed like a ninja?

Ben propped his bike against the bushes, and got ready to tail his own grandmother.

Which was one thing he had never in a million years dreamed of doing.

Like a spider scuttling around a bathroom trying not to be seen, Granny steered her scooter close to the walls. Ben followed on foot as quietly as possible. It wasn't too difficult to keep up, as the top speed of the mobility scooter was four miles per hour. Whirring across the road, she suddenly looked back as if she had heard something, and Ben dived behind a tree.

He waited, holding his breath.

Nothing.

After a few moments, he poked his head round the trunk, and saw that Granny had reached the end of the road. He continued his chase.

Soon they were near the town's high street. It was all but deserted. As it was early evening, all the shops had shut for the day and the pubs and restaurants had yet to open for the night. Granny stayed out of the glow of the streetlights, **swerving** into doorways, as she neared her destination.

Ben gasped when he saw where she had parked.

The jeweller's shop.

Necklaces and rings and watches *sparkled* in the window. Ben couldn't believe his eyes as Granny took out a tin of **cabbage** soup from the scooter's basket. She glanced around theatrically then pulled back her arm in readiness to smash the tin through the jeweller's shop window.

"Nooooo!" shouted Ben.

Granny dropped the tin. It crashed to the ground and **cabbage** soup oozed on to the pavement.

"Ben?" hissed Granny. "What are you doing here?"

9

Ben stared at his granny as she stood by the jeweller's shop, dressed all in black.

"Ben?" she prompted. "What are you doing following me?"

"I just... I..." Ben was so shocked he couldn't form a sentence.

"Well," she said. "Whatever you're doing here, you'll have the cops on us in no time. We'd better get out of here. Quick, jump on."

"But I can't—"

"Ben! We've got about thirty seconds before that CCTV camera comes on." She pointed to a camera screwed to the wall of an apartment block next to the row of shops.

Ben jumped on the back of her mobility scooter. "You know when the CCTV cameras come on?" he asked.

"Oh," said Granny, "you'd be surprised by what I know."

Ben looked at her back as she drove. He'd just seen her preparing to rob a jeweller's shop, how could he be *more* surprised? Clearly there was a lot more to his granny than he had ever known.

"Hold on," said Granny. "I'm going full throttle."

She violently twisted the handle of the scooter, to absolutely no effect that Ben could feel. They **hummed** off in the dark, going about three miles per hour with the increased weight.

*

"'The **BLACK CAT**'?" repeated Ben. They were finally back sitting in Granny's living room. She had made a pot of tea and laid out some chocolate biscuits.

"Yes, that's what they called me," replied Granny. "I was the most wanted jewel thief in the world."

Ben's head was exploding with a million questions. *Why? Where? Who? What? When?* It was impossible to know what to ask first.

"No one else knows except you, Ben," continued Granny. "Even your granddad went to his grave not knowing. Can you keep a secret? You have to swear not to tell a soul."

"But—"

Granny's face looked fierce for a moment. Her eyes narrowed and darkened like a snake about to bite.

"You have to swear," the old lady said with an

intensity Ben had never witnessed before. "Us criminals take our oaths very seriously. Very seriously *indeed*."

Ben gulped, a little scared. "I swear not to tell anyone."

"Not even your mother and father!" barked Granny, nearly spitting out her false teeth in the process.

"I said, I swear not to tell anyone," barked back Ben.

Ben had been learning about Venn diagrams in school recently. As he had sworn not to tell anyone, and let's say that "anyone" is Set A, then Mum and Dad are obviously included in Set A and are of course a subset of it, so there was really no need for Granny to ask Ben to swear a second time.

Take a look at this handy diagram:

Set A, anyone.

Set B, Mum and Dad.

But Ben didn't think his granny would be interested in Venn diagrams right now. Since she was still staring at him with those **SCARY EYES,** he sighed, and said, "All right, I swear not to tell Mum and Dad."

"Good boy," said Granny as her hearing aid began to whistle.

"Erm, on one condition," ventured Ben.

"What's that?" said Granny, seeming a little startled by his nerve.

"You have to tell me everything…"

10

EVERYTHING

"I was about your age when I stole my first diamond ring," said Granny.

Ben was astonished; partly at the idea that Granny had ever been his age, which seemed **impossible,** and partly because of the obvious fact that eleven-year-old girls do not usually steal diamonds. Glitter pens, hairclips, toy ponies maybe, diamonds definitely not.

"I know you look at me with my SCRABBLE and my knitting and my fondness for cabbage, and think I am just some boring old dear…"

"No…" said Ben, not entirely convincingly.

"But you forget, child, that I was young once."

"What was the first ring you stole?" said Ben eagerly. "Did it have a really big diamond on it?"

The old lady chuckled. "Not so big! No, it was my first one. I've still got it somewhere. Go into the kitchen, will you, Ben, and fetch the Silver Jubilee biscuit tin from the shelf."

Ben shrugged as if he knew nothing about the Silver Jubilee biscuit tin, and its incredible contents.

"Whereabouts is it, Granny?" asked Ben as he left the living room.

"Just on top of the larder, boy!" called Granny. **"Chop-chop.** Your mummy and daddy will be wondering where you are soon."

Ben remembered that he had wanted to rush home for Cheesy Beans and Sausage. Suddenly that seemed colossally unimportant. He wasn't even feeling hungry any more.

Ben re-entered the room holding the tin. It was even heavier than he remembered. He passed it to his granny.

"Good boy," she said as she rummaged through the tin, and picked out a particularly beautiful little *sparkler*.

"Aah, yes, this is it!"

To Ben, all the diamond rings looked pretty much the same. However, Granny seemed to know each of them as if they were her oldest friends.

"Such a little beauty," she said as she brought the ring up to her eye for closer inspection. "This is the first one I stole, back when I was a nipper."

Ben couldn't imagine what Granny would have been like young. He had only known her as an old lady. He even imagined she had been born an old lady. That years ago in the hospital when her mother had given birth and asked the midwife if it was a boy or a girl, the midwife might have replied, *"It's an old lady!"*

"I grew up in a small village, and my family were very poor," continued Granny. "And up at the top of the hill was this grand country house where a Lord and Lady lived. Lord and Lady Davenport. It was just after the war and we didn't have much food in those days. I was hungry, so one night at midnight, when everyone was asleep I crept out of my mother and father's little cottage. Under the cover of darkness, I made my way through the woods and up the hill to Davenport House."

"Weren't you scared?" asked Ben.

"Yes, of course I was. Being alone in the dark woods at night, it was **TERRIFYING.** There were guard dogs at the house. Great big black Dobermans. So as quietly as I could, I climbed a drainpipe and found an unlocked window. I was a very little girl at eleven, small for my age. So I managed to squeeze myself through a tiny gap in the window, and landed behind a velvet curtain. When I pulled back the curtain I realised I was in Lord and Lady Davenport's bedroom."

"Oh no!" said Ben.

"Oh yes," continued the old lady. "I thought I might just take some food, perhaps, but next to the bed I saw this little beauty."

She indicated the diamond ring.

"So you just took it?"

"Being an international jewel thief is never that simple, young man," said Granny. "The Lord and Lady were snoring heavily, but if I woke them I'd be dead. The Lord always slept with a shotgun by the bed."

"A shotgun?" asked Ben.

"Yes, he was posh, and being posh he liked hunting pheasants, so he owned many guns."

Ben was sweating with nerves. "But he didn't wake up and try and shoot you, did he?"

"Be patient, young man. All in good time. I crept over to Lady Davenport's side of the bed and picked up the diamond ring. I couldn't believe how beautiful it was. I had never seen one up close before. My mother would never have dreamed of owning one. 'I don't need jewels,' she would say to us children. '*You* are my little diamonds.' I wondered at the diamond in my hand for a moment. It was the most gorgeous thing I had ever seen in my life. Then, suddenly, there was an almighty noise." Ben frowned. "What was it?"

"Lord Davenport was a big fat greedy man. He must have had too much to eat earlier because he let out the most enormous burp!"

Ben laughed and Granny laughed too. He knew burps weren't supposed to be funny, but couldn't help laughing.

"It was so loud!" said Granny, still chuckling.

"BBBBBBBBBB BBUUUUUUUUUU UUUUURRRRRR RRRRRRRPPPP PPPPPPPP!!!!!!!!!"

she mimicked.

Ben was helpless with laughter now.

"It was so loud," continued Granny, "that I was startled and dropped the ring on the polished wooden floor. It made quite a **bang** as it hit the teak, and both Lord and Lady Davenport woke up."

"Oh no!"

"Oh yes! So I grabbed the ring and ran back to the open window. I didn't dare look behind me, as I could hear Lord Davenport cocking his shotgun. I leaped down on to the grass, and all of a sudden the lights in the house came on and the dogs were barking and I was running for my life. Then I heard a deafening sound…"

"Another burp?" asked Ben.

"No, a gunshot this time. Lord Davenport was shooting at me as I ran down the hill and back to the woods."

"Then what happened?"

Granny looked at her little gold watch. "My dear, you had better head home. Your mummy and daddy will be worried sick."

"I doubt it," said Ben. "All they care about is stupid **ballroom dancing.**"

"That's not true," said Granny unexpectedly. "You know they love you."

"I want to hear the end of the story," said Ben, frustrated. He was desperate to know what happened next.

"You will. Another day."

"But, Granny…"

"Ben, you have to go home."

"That's not fair!"

"Ben, you must leave now. I can tell you what happened when you come another day."

"BUT!"

"To be continued," she said.

11

CHEESY BEANS
AND
SAUSAGE

Ben sped home on his bike, not even noticing his burning legs and aching chest. He was going so fast he thought the police might give him a speeding ticket. As the wheels raced round so did his mind.

Could his boring old granny really be a gangsta?!

A **gangsta granny?***!*

That must be why she liked books about gangstas so much – she was one!

He slid through the back door just as the familiar **STRICTLY STARS DANCING** theme tune blasted out from the living room. He had made it home just in time.

But as Ben was about to disappear upstairs and pretend he had been in his bedroom doing his homework, Mum burst into the kitchen.

"What are you doing?" she asked suspiciously. "You look very sweaty."

"Oh, nothing," said Ben, feeling very sweaty.

"Look at you," she continued, as she approached him. "You are sweating like a pig."

Ben had seen a few pigs in his life and none of them had been sweating. In fact, pig fans everywhere will tell you that pigs don't even have sweat glands, so they can't sweat.

Wow, this book is actually really educational.

"I'm not sweating," Ben protested. Being accused of sweating made him sweat even more.

"You *are* sweating. Have you been out running?"

"No," replied a now very sweaty Ben.

"Ben, don't lie to me, I'm your mother," she said, pointing at herself, a false nail flying off into the air in the process.

Her false nails came off a lot. Once Ben had even found one in his microwaveable paella Bolognese.

"If you haven't been out running, Ben, then why are you sweating?"

Ben had to think fast. The **STRICTLY STARS DANCING** theme tune was coming to an end.

"I was dancing!" he blurted out.

"Dancing?" Mum didn't look convinced. Ben was no **Flavio Flavioli**. And of course he hated **ballroom dancing.**

"Yes, well, I have changed my mind about **ballroom dancing.** I love it!"

"But you said you hated it," shot back an increasingly suspicious Mum. "Many many

many times. Only the other week you said that you would rather 'eat your own bogeys than watch that rubbish'. Hearing you say that was like a dagger through my heart!"

Mum was becoming visibly upset at the memory.

"I'm sorry, Mum, I really am."

Ben reached out a hand to comfort her and another false nail fell on to the floor. "But now I love it, honestly. I was just watching STRICTLY through the crack in the door, and copying all the moves."

Mum beamed with pride. She looked as if her whole life suddenly had meaning. Her face turned strangely happy yet sad, as if this was destiny.

"Do you want to be a…" She took a deep breath, "…professional dancer?"

"Where's my Cheesy Beans and Sausage,

wife?!" called Dad from the living room.

"Shut your face, Pete!" Mum's eyes were wet with tears of joy.

She hadn't cried so much since **Flavio** was kicked out of the show in week two last year. **Flavio** had been forced to partner Dame Rachel Prejudice, who was so podgy all he could do was drag her around the floor.

"Well... erm... aah..." Ben desperately searched for a way to get out of this one. "...yeah."

That really wasn't it.

"Yes! I knew it!" cried Mum. "Pete, come in here a moment. Ben has got something he needs to tell you."

Dad trudged in wearily. "What is it, Ben? You're not joining the circus, are you? My word, you are sweaty."

"No, Pete," said Mum, slowly and deliberately

as if she was about to read out the name of a winner at an awards ceremony. "Ben doesn't want to be a silly old plumber any more—"

"Thank goodness for that," said Dad.

"He wants to be…" Mum looked at her son. "Tell him, Ben."

Ben opened his mouth, but before he could say anything Mum chimed in. "Ben wants to be a **ballroom dancer!**"

"Oh, there is a God!" exclaimed Dad. He looked up at the nicotine-stained ceiling as if he might catch a glimpse of the divine one.

"He was just practising in the kitchen," jabbered Mum excitedly. "Copying all the moves from the show…"

Dad looked into his son's eyes and shook his hand manfully. "That's wonderful news, my boy! Your mum and me haven't achieved much in our lives. What with Mum being a nail polisher—"

"I am a nail technician, Pete!" corrected Mum scornfully. "There is a world of difference, Pete, you do know that…"

"Nail technician. Sorry. And me being just a boring old security guard because I was too fat for the police. The most excitement I've had all year was when I stopped a man in a wheelchair speeding out of the store with a tin of custard concealed under his blanket. But you becoming a ballroom dancer, well... this... this is the greatest thing that's ever happened to us."

"The very greatest!" said Mum.

"The very very greatest," agreed Dad.

"Really it's the very very very greatest," said Mum.

"Let's just agree it's extremely great," said Dad, irritated. "Only, I warn you, boy, it's not going to be easy. If you train eight hours a day every day for the next twenty years, you might just get on the TV show."

"Maybe he can do the American version!" exclaimed Mum. "Oh, Pete, just imagine, our boy a huge star in **AMERICA!**"

"Well, let's not jump the gun, wife. He's not won the British one yet. Right now we have to think about entering him for a junior competition."

"You're right, Pete. Gail told me there's one in the town hall just before Christmas."

"Crack open the sparkling wine, wife! Our son is going to be a *cha-cha-cha champion!*"

A naughty word exploded in Ben's head.

How on earth was he going to get out of this?!

12

THE LOVE BOMB

Ben had spent the whole of Sunday morning being measured up by Mum for his dance outfit. She had stayed up through the night, sketching possible designs.

Under duress, he was forced to choose one, and pointed a limp finger at the one that he thought was the least hideous.

Mum's hand-drawn options ranged all the way from the embarrassing to the humiliating…

There was:

The Woodland

Fruit Cocktail

Thunder and Lightning

Accident and Emergency

Ice and a Slice

The Hedgerow and Badger

The Quality Street

Eggs 'n' Bacon

Confetti

The Underwater World

Burning Love

Cheese and Pickle

The Solar System

Piano Man

But the one that Ben thought was the *least* worst... was the **LOVE Bomb**:

"We will have to find you a nice young girl to partner with for the competition!" said Mum, excitedly, as she accidentally ran one of her fake nails under the sewing machine and it exploded.

Ben hadn't thought about dance partners.

Not only was he going to have to dance, he was going to have to dance with a girl! And not just any girl, but a revoltingly precocious sparkly fake-tanned leotard-wearing over-made-up one.

Ben was still at the age when he thought girls were as appealing as **frogspawn**.

"Oh, I'm just going to dance on my own," he spluttered.

"A solo piece!" exclaimed Mum. "How original!"

"In fact, I can't stand here talking all day. I'd better go and practise," said Ben, as he disappeared upstairs to his room. He shut the door, turned on his radio, and then climbed out of the window and raced over to Granny's bungalow on his bike.

"So, you were running off into the woods, when Lord Davenport started shooting at you…" Ben was eagerly prompting his granny.

But for the moment her mind was blank.

"Was I?" said Granny, looking increasingly befuddled.

"That's where the story ended last night. You said you had snatched the ring from the Davenports' bedroom, and were running across the lawn when you heard shots…"

"Oh yes, yes," muttered Granny, her face suddenly illuminated.

Ben smiled broadly. He suddenly remembered how he had used to love his granny telling stories when he was younger, transporting him to a magical world. A world where you paint pictures in your mind that are more thrilling than all the movies or TV shows or video games in the universe.

Only a couple of weeks ago he had pretended to be asleep to stop her telling him a bedtime story. Clearly he'd forgotten how thrilling stories could be.

"I was running and running," continued Granny breathlessly, as if she was actually running, "and I heard a shot ring out. Then another. I knew from the sound that it was definitely a shotgun rather than a rifle—"

"What's the difference?" asked Ben.

"Well, a rifle shoots one bullet and is more accurate. But a shotgun sprays hundreds of little deadly balls of lead. Any idiot can hit you if they fire a shotgun in your direction."

"And did he?" said Ben. His smile had faded now. He was genuinely worried.

"Yes, but luckily I was far away by then so I was only grazed. I could hear the dogs barking too. They were hunting me; and I was only a small girl. If they had caught me, the hounds would have ripped me to shreds..."

Ben gasped in horror. "So how did you get away?" he asked.

"I took a chance. I couldn't outrun the dogs through the forest. The fastest runner in the world couldn't. But I knew the woods really well. I used to play in them for hours with my brothers and sisters. I knew if I could just get across the stream, then the dogs would lose the scent."

"How come?"

"Dogs can't follow a scent across water. And there was a great oak tree just on the other side of the stream. If I climbed that tree, I might be safe."

Ben couldn't imagine his granny climbing stairs, let alone a tree. She had lived in her bungalow ever since he could remember.

"More shots rang out through the darkness as I ran towards the stream," continued the old lady. "And I stumbled in the gloom of the forest. I tripped on a tree root and fell **face first** in the mud. Scrambling to my feet, I turned round to see an army of men on horseback led by Lord Davenport. They were carrying flaming torches and holding shotguns. The whole forest was lit up with the fire from the torches. I jumped into the stream. It was around this time of year; in the depth of winter and the water was icy. The cold shocked me and I could hardly breathe. I clapped my hand over my mouth to stifle a

scream. I could hear the dogs getting nearer and nearer, barking and barking. There must have been dozens of them. I looked behind me and I could see their sharp teeth gleaming in the moonlight.

"So I waded across the stream and started climbing the tree. My hands were muddy, and my legs and feet were wet, and I kept slipping down the trunk. I frantically rubbed my hands on my nightshirt and began to climb again. I scrambled to the very top of the tree and stayed as still as I could. I heard the dogs and the army of Davenport's men follow the stream down to a different part of the forest. The dogs' ferocious barks became distant and after a while the torches were just specks in the distance. I was safe. I shivered up that tree for hours. I waited until dawn, slid down the tree, and made my way back to our cottage. I crept into bed and lay there for a few moments before the sun rose."

Ben could picture everything she described perfectly in his mind. Granny had him utterly spellbound.

"Did they come looking for you?" he asked.

"Well, no one got a good-enough look at me, so Davenport had his men search everywhere in the village. Every cottage was turned upside down to look for the ring."

"Didn't you say anything?"

"I wanted to. I felt so guilty. But I knew if I owned up I would be in deep trouble. Lord Davenport would have had me publicly flogged in the village square."

"So what did you do?"

"I... swallowed it."

Ben couldn't believe his ears. "The ring, Granny? You swallowed the ring?"

"I thought it was the best way to hide it. In

my stomach. A few days later it came out when I went to the toilet."

"That must have been painful!" said Ben, his bum wincing at the thought. Passing a big diamond ring out of his bottom didn't sound in any way enjoyable.

"It was painful. Excruciating, in fact." Granny grimaced. "The good thing was that our cottage had been searched already from top to bottom – not *my* bottom – the bottom of the cottage, I mean…" Ben chuckled. "…and Davenport's men had moved on to searching the next village. So one night I went off into the woods and hid the ring. I placed it where no one would ever look; under a rock in the stream."

"Clever!" said Ben.

"But that ring was only the first of many, Ben. Stealing it had been the biggest thrill of my life. And as I lay in bed each night, all I dreamed about was stealing more and more diamonds. That ring was just the beginning..." continued Granny in a low whisper, staring deep into Ben's innocent young eyes, "...of a lifetime of crime."

13

A LIFETIME OF CRIME

Hours passed in what seemed like minutes, as Granny told her grandson how she had stolen every one of the dazzling items spread out on the living-room floor.

The huge tiara had belonged to the wife of the President of the United States of America, the First Lady. Granny told Ben how, over fifty years earlier, she had sailed all the way to America on a cruise liner to steal it from the White House in Washington. And that while sailing back home she had robbed every rich lady on the ship of her jewels! How she was caught red-handed by

the captain of the ship and escaped by diving overboard and swimming the last few miles of the Atlantic Ocean back to England with all of the jewellery hidden in her knickers.

Granny told Ben that the sparkling emerald
earrings that had been in her little bungalow
for decades were worth over a million
pounds each. They had once belonged

to the wife of an enormously wealthy Indian maharajah, a maharani. The old lady recounted how she enlisted the help of a herd of elephants to steal them. She had coaxed the elephants to stand on top of each other to form a giant ladder so she could scale the wall of the fort in India where the earrings were kept in the royal bedchamber.

The most amazing tale of all was of how she stole the **enormous** deep blue sapphire and diamond brooch that sat sparkling on her worn living-room carpet. She told Ben that it had once belonged to the last Empress of Russia, who ruled with her husband the Tsar before the Communist revolution of 1917. It had for many years been under bulletproof glass at the Hermitage museum in St Petersburg, guarded twenty-four hours a day, seven days a week, three hundred and sixty-five days a year by a platoon of fearsome Russian soldiers.

This theft had required the most elaborate plan of all. Granny had hidden in an ancient suit of armour in the museum, which dated back hundreds of years to the time of Catherine the Great. Each time the soldiers looked the other way, she would edge forward in the metal suit a few millimetres, until she got close enough to the brooch. It took her a week.

"What, like Granny's Footsteps?" asked Ben.

"Exactly, young man!" she replied. "Then I smashed the glass with the silver axe I was holding and grabbed the brooch."

"How did you escape, Granny?"

"That's a good question… now, how did I escape?" Granny looked flummoxed. "Sorry, it's my age, boy. I forget things."

Ben smiled supportively. "That's OK, Granny."

Soon the old lady's memory seemed to come back into focus. "Oh yes, I remember," she continued. "I ran outside into the courtyard of the museum, leaped into the barrel of a huge cannon and then *fired* myself to safety!"

Ben pictured this for a moment: his granny, in deepest darkest Russia, flying through the air in an ancient suit of armour. It was hard to believe, but how else could this little old lady come to have such an astonishing collection of priceless gems?

Ben loved Granny's daring tales. At home, Ben had never had stories read or told to him. His parents always just switched on the television and slumped down on the sofa when they got home from work. Hearing the old lady talk was so exciting Ben wished he could move in with her. He could listen to Granny all day.

"There can't be a jewel in the world you

haven't stolen!" said Ben.

"Oh yes, there is, young man. Hang on, what's that?"

"What's what?" said Ben.

Granny was pointing behind Ben's head, an expression of horror on her face. "It's… It's…"

"*What?*" said Ben, not daring to turn round and see what she was pointing at. A shiver ran down his spine.

"Whatever you do," said Granny, "don't turn round…"

14

NOSY NEIGHBOUR

Ben couldn't help himself, and his eyes darted towards the window. For a brief moment he saw a dark figure wearing a strange hat peer through the dirty glass, and then quickly disappear out of view.

"There was a man peering in at the window," said Ben breathlessly.

"I know," said Granny. "I told you not to look."

"Shall I go out and see who it was?" said Ben, trying to hide the fact that he was more than a little frightened. Really, he wanted Granny to go out and see who it was.

"I bet it was my nosy neighbour, Mr Parker. He lives at number seven, he always wears a pork-pie hat, and he keeps spying on me."

"Why?" asked Ben.

Granny shrugged. "I don't know. I imagine he has a rather cold head, or something."

"What?" said Ben. "Oh. No, not his hat. I mean, why does he keep spying on you?"

"He's a retired Major, and now he runs the Neighbourhood Watch scheme in GREY CLOSE."

"What's Neighbourhood Watch?" asked Ben.

"It's a group of local people who keep an eye out for burglars. But Mr Parker just uses it as an excuse to spy on everyone, the nosy old git. I often come back from the supermarket with my bag of cabbages and see he's hiding behind his net curtains, spying on me with a pair of binoculars."

"Is he suspicious about you?" said Ben, more

than a little panicked. He didn't want to be thrown in jail for aiding and abetting a criminal. He didn't really know what "abetting" meant, actually, but he knew it was a crime, and he knew he was too young for prison.

"He is suspicious about everyone. We have to keep an eye out for him, young lad. The man is a menace."

Ben went over to the window and peered out. He couldn't see anyone.

BBBBBRRRRRRRRRIIIIIIIIIINNNNNNNNNGGGG GGGGGGGG!!!!!!!!!!!!!!!!!!!!!!!!

Ben's heart missed a beat. It was only the doorbell, but if they let Mr Parker inside he would see all the evidence the police would need to send Ben and his granny straight to prison.

"Don't answer it!" said Ben, as he ran to the middle of the room and started stuffing all the jewels back in the tin, as quickly as he could.

"What do you mean, don't answer it?! He knows I am at home. He just saw us through the window. You answer the door and I will hide the jewels."

"Me?"

"Yes, you! Hurry!"

BBBBBBBBBBRRRRRRRRRR RIIIIIIIIIIINNNNNNNNNNNNNGGGGG GGGG!!!!!!!!!!!!!!!!!!!!!!!!!!!!!!!!!!!! !!!!!!!!!!!!!

This ring was more insistent. Mr Parker had left his finger on the buzzer for even longer. Ben took a deep breath and walked calmly through the hall to the front door.

He opened it.

Outside stood a man in a very silly hat. Don't believe me? This is how silly his hat was:

"Yes?" said Ben in a squeaky high voice. "Can I help you?"

Mr Parker put his foot inside the bungalow so the front door couldn't be closed on him.

"Who are you?" he barked, nasally.

He had a very big nose, which made him

seem even nosier than he was, and he already seemed extremely nosy. Because he had a big nose he also had a very nasal voice, which made everything he said, however serious, seem a little bit absurd. But his eyes shone red like a demon's.

"I am Granny's friend," spluttered Ben. *Why did I say that?* he thought. In truth, he was in a terrible panic, and his tongue was running away with him.

"Friend?" snarled Mr Parker, pushing open the front door. He was stronger than Ben, and soon forced his way inside.

"I mean grandson, Mr Parker, sir…" said Ben, retreating towards the living room.

"Why are you lying to me?" he said, taking several paces forward as Ben took several paces back. It was as if they were dancing the tango.

"I am not lying!" cried Ben.

They reached the living-room door.

"You can't go in there!" yelled Ben, thinking of the jewels still scattered all over the carpet.

"Why not?"

"Erm… umm… Because Granny is doing her naked yoga!"

Ben needed a **DRAMATIC** excuse to stop Mr Parker barging through the door and seeing the jewels. He was pretty sure he had hit the jackpot as Mr Parker paused and furrowed his brow.

Sadly, the nosy neighbour was not convinced.

"Naked yoga?! A likely story! I need to talk to your grandmother right away. Now get out of my way, you nasty little worm of a boy!" he said as he shoved the boy aside and opened the living-room door.

Granny must have heard Ben through the door because when Mr Parker burst into the room she was standing in her bra and knickers in a tree pose.

"Mr Parker, do you mind?" said Granny, in mock horror that he had seen her in a state of undress.

Mr Parker's eyes spun around the room. He didn't know where to look, so he fixed his glare on the now bare carpet. "Excuse me, Madam, but I need to ask you, where are those jewels I saw a moment ago?"

Ben spied the Silver Jubilee biscuit tin poking out from behind the sofa. Surreptitiously he edged it out of view with his foot.

"What jewels, Mr Parker? Have you been **spying** on me again?" demanded Granny, still in her underwear.

"Well, I, err…" he **spluttered.** "I had good reason. I was suspicious when I saw a young gentleman enter your property. I thought he might be a burglar."

"I let him in through the front door."

"He might have been a very charming burglar. He might have weaselled his way into your confidence."

"He's my grandson. He stays every Friday night."

"Ah!" said Mr Parker triumphantly. "But it's not Friday night! So you can see why my suspicions were raised. And as head of **GREY CLOSE'S Neighbourhood Watch** I must report anything suspicious I see to the police."

"I've got a good mind to report you to the police, Mr Parker!" said Ben.

Granny looked at him curiously.

"Whatever for?" said the man. His eyes narrowed. They were now so red it was like there was a fire in his brain.

"For spying on old ladies in their underwear!" said Ben triumphantly. Granny winked at Ben.

"She was fully clothed when I looked through the window…" protested Mr Parker.

"That's what they all say!" said Granny. "Now get out of my house before you are arrested for being a peeping Tom!"

"You've not heard the last of me. Good day!" said Mr Parker. With that, he spun on his heel and left the room. Granny and Ben heard the front door **SLAM** behind him and they ran over to the window and watched him scuttle back to his bungalow.

"I think we frightened him off," said Ben.

"But he'll be back," said Granny. "We have to be very careful."

"Yes," said Ben, more than a little alarmed. "We'd better hide this tin somewhere else."

Granny thought for a moment. "Yes, I'll put it under the floorboards."

"OK," said Ben. "But first…"

"Yes, Ben?"

"You might want to get dressed."

15

RECKLESS
AND
THRILLING

When Granny had put her clothes back on, she and Ben sat down on the sofa.

"Granny, before Mr Parker turned up you were telling me there was one jewel that you never stole," Ben whispered.

"There is something quite special that every great thief in the world would love to get their hands on. But it's impossible. It just can't be done."

"I bet you could do it, Granny. You're the greatest thief the world has ever known."

"Thank you, Ben, perhaps I am, or rather

was… and stealing these particular jewels might be every great thief's dream, but it would just be, well… impossible."

"Jewels? There's more than one?"

"Yes, my dear. The last time anyone tried to steal them was three hundred years ago. A Captain Blood, I believe. And I am not sure the Queen would be pleased…" She chuckled.

"You don't mean…?"

"*The Crown Jewels*, yes, my boy."

Ben had learned about the *Crown Jewels* in a History lesson at school. History was one of the few subjects he liked, mainly because of all the gory punishments they used to have in the olden days. **"Hung, drawn and quartered"** was his absolute favourite, but he also liked the breaking wheel, being burned at the stake, and of course a red-hot poker up the bum.

Who doesn't?

At school, Ben had learned that the *Crown Jewels* were in fact a set of crowns, swords, sceptres, rings, bracelets and orbs, some of which were nearly a thousand years old. They were used when a new king or queen was crowned, and since 1303 (the year, not the time), they had been kept under lock and key in the Tower of London.

Ben had begged his parents to take him to see them, but they had moaned that London was too far away (even though it wasn't that far).

To be honest, they never really went anywhere as a family. When he was younger, Ben used to listen in silent wonder to his classmates, as they recounted their myriad adventures in "show and tell". Trips to the seaside, visits to museums, even holidays abroad. The knot in his stomach would tighten when his turn came. He was too embarrassed to admit that all he had done during the holidays was eat microwaveable meals and watch TV, so he would make up stories about flying kites and climbing trees and exploring castles.

But now he had the greatest "show and tell" of all time. His granny was an international jewel thief. A gangsta! Except if he showed or told this, the old dear would be put in prison and they would throw away the key.

Ben realised that this was his big chance to do something crazy and reckless and thrilling.

"I can help you," said Ben in a cool and calm manner, though his heart was beating faster than ever.

"Help me do what?" replied the old lady, a little befuddled.

"Steal the *Crown Jewels*, of course!" said Ben.

16

"N" AND "O" SPELLS "NO"

"No!" shouted Granny as her hearing aid began whistling furiously.

"Yes!" shouted Ben.

"No!"

"Yes!"

"Nooo!"

"Yeeees!"

"NOOOOOOOOOOOOOOOOOOO OOOOOOOOOOOOOOOOO!"

"YEEEEEEEEEEEEEEEEEEEEEE EEEEEEEEEEEEES!"

This went on for a few minutes, but to save

paper and therefore the trees and therefore the forests and therefore the environment and therefore the world, I have tried to keep it short.

"There is absolutely no way I am letting a boy of your age come on a heist with me! Especially not to steal the *Crown Jewels!* And most important of all, it's impossible! It can't be done!" exclaimed Granny.

"There must be a way…" pleaded Ben.

"Ben, I said 'no' and that's final!"

"But—"

"No buts, Ben. No. 'N' and 'O' spells 'no'."

Ben was bitterly disappointed, but the lady was not for turning. "I'd better go then," he said despondently.

Granny looked a little downcast too. "Yes, dear, you'd better – your mummy and daddy will be very worried about you."

"They won't be—"

"Ben! Home! Now!"

Ben was sad to see that Granny was becoming like one of the boring grown-ups again, just when she'd started to become interesting. Still, he did what she said. Apart from anything else, he didn't want to make his parents suspicious, so he raced home and climbed up the drainpipe to his bedroom window, before rushing downstairs to the living room.

Unsurprisingly, though, Mum and Dad hadn't been worried about where Ben was at all. They had been too busy planning their son's rise to dancing **SUPERSTARDOM** to notice he was gone.

Dad had been calling and calling the national under-twelve dance competition hotline until finally he got through and secured his son a place. Mum was right, the competition was at the town hall in just a couple of weeks' time. There was no time to lose, so Mum had been working every waking moment on her son's **Love Bomb** outfit.

"How's the rehearsals going, boy?" asked Dad. "You look like you've worked up quite a sweat."

"Fine, thank you, Dad," lied Ben. "I really am getting something spectacular together for the big night."

Ben cursed his runaway mouth.

Something spectacular?

He'd be lucky if he didn't fall over and knock himself out.

"Well, we can't wait to see it! Not long to go!" said Mum, not even looking up from the sewing machine, as she stitched a row of hundreds of sparkling red hearts down the side of his

Lycra trousers.

"I'd kind of like to practise on my own for now, Mum, you know..." Ben gulped nervously. "Until it's completely ready to show you."

"Yes, yes, we understand," said Mum.

Ben sighed with relief. He had bought himself a bit more time.

But only a little bit.

In a couple of weeks Ben was still going to have to perform a solo dance routine for the whole town.

He sat on his bed, and reached underneath it for his stash of **PLUMBING WEEKLY**s. Flicking through an issue from the previous year, he saw that it contained a feature entitled "A Short History of Plumbing" that focused on some of London's oldest sewage pipes. Ben frantically turned the pages to find it.

Eureka! There it was.

Hundreds of years ago the River Thames, on the banks of which the Tower of London is situated, had been an open sewer. (Technically speaking, that means there was a lot of wee and poo in it.)

Buildings along the riverside simply had big pipes leading from their toilets straight into the river. In the magazine were detailed historical diagrams of various famous buildings in London, showing where their old sewage pipes connected to the river.

And…

Ben's finger ran down the article…

Yes! A chart of the sewer pipes at the Tower of London.

This could be the key to stealing the *Crown Jewels*. One pipe was nearly a metre wide, big enough for a child to swim up. And maybe big enough for a little old lady too!

The article also said that, when the plumbing systems were modernised and proper sewers installed a lot of the old pipes were simply left where they were, because it was simpler than digging them up.

Ben's head spun as he thought about what this meant. It was possible – just possible

– that there was still a huge pipe leading from the Thames into the Tower of London, and that most people, apart from very keen plumbing enthusiasts, had forgotten it was there. Ben wouldn't have known himself, if he hadn't been a long-term subscriber to **PLUMBING WEEKLY**.

He and Granny could swim up that pipe, and get into the Tower…

Mum and Dad were wrong! he thought. *Plumbing can be exciting.*

Of course, it was a sewage pipe, which wasn't ideal, but any poo and wee still in it would be hundreds of years old.

Ben didn't know if that was a good or bad thing.

At that moment, he heard a creak in the floorboards and his bedroom door flew open. His mum burst in holding a big piece of Lycra that looked ominously like his **"Love Bomb"** outfit.

Ben quickly concealed the magazine under his bed, which made him look incredibly guilty.

"I was just going to get you to try this on," said Mum.

"Oh yes," said Ben, as he sat on his bed awkwardly, his heels pushing the remaining **PLUMBING WEEKLY**s out of sight of Mum's prying eyes.

"What's that?" she said. "What did you hide when I came in? Is that a rude magazine?"

"No," said Ben, swallowing his guilt. This looked way worse than it was. It looked like he was hiding a naughty magazine under the bed.

"It's nothing to be ashamed of, Ben. I think it's healthy you are expressing an interest in girls."

Oh no! thought Ben. *My mum's going to talk to me about girls!*

"There's nothing embarrassing about being interested in girls, Ben."

"Yes there is! Girls are **gross!**"

"No, Ben, it's the most natural thing in the world…"

She's just not stopping!

"THE DINNER IS NEARLY READY, LOVE!" came a shout from downstairs. "WHAT ARE YOU DOING UP THERE?"

"I AM TALKING TO BEN ABOUT GIRLS!" Mum shouted back.

Ben was so red that if he opened his mouth wide enough he might be mistaken for a postbox.

"WHAT?" cried Dad.

"GIRLS!" shouted Mum. "I AM TALKING TO OUR SON ABOUT GIRLS!"

"OH, RIGHT!" Dad shouted back. "I'LL TURN THE OVEN OFF."

"So, Ben, if you ever need to—"

BRING BRING. BRING BRING.

It was Mum's mobile phone going off in her pocket.

"Sorry, dear," she said, placing the handset to her ear. "Gail, can I call you back? I am just talking to Ben about girls. OK, thanks, bub-bye."

She hung up the phone and turned to Ben.

"Sorry, where was I? Oh yes, if you ever need to have a little chat with me about girls, then please do. You can trust me to be very discreet..."

17

PLANNING THE HEIST

For the first time in his life, Ben *skipped* to school the following morning.

Through his love of plumbing, the previous night he had discovered that the Tower of London had a weakness. The most impregnable building in the world, where some of the country's most dangerous criminals had been imprisoned and executed, had a **FATAL FLAW:** a large sewage pipe that led directly into the River Thames.

That ancient tube would be his and Granny's way in and out of the Tower! It was a quite brilliant plan, and Ben's body couldn't hide its excitement at this amazing discovery.

That's why he was skipping.

Now he couldn't wait until Friday night when his mum and dad would once again pack him off to Granny's.

Then he would be able to convince the old lady that together they really could steal the *Crown Jewels*. Ben would bring along the diagram in **PLUMBING WEEKLY** of the Tower of London's sewage system to show her. The two of them could stay up all night and work out every detail of the most daring robbery of all time.

The problem was that a whole fat week of lessons and teachers and homework stood between now and Friday night. However, Ben was determined to use the week at school wisely.

In his IT lesson, he looked up the *Crown Jewels* and memorised every detail on the web page.

In History, he asked his teacher questions about the Tower of London and exactly where in the building the jewels were kept. (That would be the Jewel House, fact fans.)

In Geography, he found an atlas of the British Isles and pinpointed precisely where on the Thames the Tower is situated.

In PE, he didn't accidentally on purpose forget his kit like usual, instead he did extra press-ups so his arms would be strong enough to pull himself up the sewage pipe that led into the Tower.

In Maths, he asked the teacher how many packets of Rolos you could buy with five billion pounds (which is what the *Crown Jewels* were said to be worth). Rolos were Ben's absolute favourite sweets.

The answer is ten billion packets, or twenty-four billion actual Rolos. That's enough for a year at least.

And Raj was sure to throw in a few extra packets for free.

In his French class, Ben learned how to say, *"I know nothing about the theft of, how you say, 'the Crown Jewels', I am but a poor French peasant boy,"* in case he needed to pretend he was a poor French peasant boy in order to escape from the scene of the crime.

In Spanish he learned to say, *"I know nothing about, how you say, 'the Crown Jewels', I am but a poor Spanish peasant boy,"* in case he needed to pretend he was a poor Spanish peasant boy in order to escape from the scene of the crime.

In German he learned to say… well, I'm sure you get the idea.

In Science, Ben quizzed his teacher about how you might be able to penetrate bulletproof glass. Even if you got into the Jewel House, removing the jewels was not going to be easy, as they were kept behind glass that was inches thick.

In his Art class, he made a detailed scale model of the Tower of London out of matches so he could role-play the daring robbery in miniature.

The week absolutely flew by – never had school been so much fun. Most importantly, for the first time in his life Ben couldn't wait to spend time with his granny.

By the end of school on Friday afternoon, Ben felt he had all the data he needed to put the daring plan into place.

The story of the theft of the *Crown Jewels* would be on the TV news for weeks, on every website, and emblazoned across every front page of every newspaper in every country in the world. However, no one, but no one, would suspect that the thieves were in fact a little old lady and an eleven-year-old boy. They were going to get away with the crime of the century!

18

VISITING HOURS

"You can't stay with Granny tonight," said Dad. It was four o'clock on Friday afternoon, and Ben had just got home from school. It was strange that Dad was home so early. He usually didn't finish his shift at the supermarket until eight.

"Why not?" asked Ben, noticing his dad's face was dark with worry.

"I'm afraid I've got some bad news, son."

"What?" demanded Ben, his face darkening with worry too.

"Granny's in hospital."

*

A little while later, once they'd finally found a parking space, Ben and his parents went through the automatic doors of the hospital. Ben wondered if Mum and Dad were ever going to find Granny in here. The hospital was impossibly tall and wide, a great monument to illness.

There were lifts that took you to other lifts.

Mile-long corridors.

Signs everywhere that Ben couldn't comprehend:

CORONARY CARE UNIT

RADIOLOGY

OBSTETRICS

CLINICAL DECISION UNIT

MRI SCANNING ROOM

Confused-looking patients on trolleys or in wheelchairs were being wheeled up and down by porters, as doctors and nurses, who looked like they hadn't been to bed for days, hurried past them.

When they finally found the wing Granny was in, right up on the nineteenth floor, Ben didn't recognise her at first.

Her hair was flat on her head, she didn't have her glasses on or her teeth in, and she was wearing not her own clothes, but a standard issue NHS nightgown. It was as if all of the things that made her Granny had been taken from her, and she was now just a shell.

Ben felt so sad to see her like this, but tried to hide it. He didn't want to upset her.

"Hello, dears," she said. Her voice was croaky, and her speech a little slurred. Ben had to take a deep breath to stop from bursting into tears.

"How are you feeling, Mum?" asked Ben's dad.

"Not too clever," she replied. "I had a fall."

"A fall?" said Ben.

"Yes. I don't remember much about it. One moment I was reaching in the larder for a tin of cabbage soup, the next thing I knew I was lying on the lino staring at the ceiling. My cousin Edna called me a number of times from her nursing home. When she couldn't get an answer, she called an ambulance."

"When did you fall over, Granny?" asked Ben.

"Let me think, I was lying on the kitchen floor for two days, so it must have been Wednesday morning. I couldn't get up to reach the telephone."

"I am so sorry, Mum," said Dad quietly. Ben had never seen his father look so upset.

"It's funny, because I meant to call you on Wednesday, you know just for a chat, to see how you are," said Mum, lying. She had never called the old lady in her life, and if Granny ever called the house Mum couldn't get off the phone quick enough.

"You weren't to know, my dear," said Granny. "They did all kinds of tests this morning to see what's wrong with me; X-rays and scans and the like. I'll get the results tomorrow. Hopefully I won't be in here too long."

"I hope so too," said Ben.

There was an uncomfortable silence.

No one quite knew what to say or do.

Mum hesitantly nudged Dad and mimed looking at her watch.

Ben knew hospitals made her uncomfortable. When he'd had his appendix out two years before she had only visited him a couple of times, and even then it had made her **sweat** and **fidget.**

"Well, we'd better be off," said Dad.

"Yes, yes, you go," said Granny, with lightness in her voice but sadness in her eyes. "Don't you worry about me, I'll be fine."

"Can't we stay a bit longer?" piped up Ben.

Mum shot him an anguished look, which Dad clocked.

"No, come along, Ben, your granny will need to go to sleep in a few hours," said Dad, as he stood up and readied himself to leave. "I'm quite busy, Mum, but I'll try and pop in over the weekend."

He patted his mother on the head, like one might a dog. It was an awkward gesture; Dad wasn't a hugger.

He turned to go. Mum smiled weakly, and

then pulled a reluctant Ben across the ward by his wrist.

Up in his bedroom, later that evening, Ben determinedly sorted all the information he'd gathered from school that week.

We'll show them, Granny, he thought fiercely. *I'm going to do it for you.* Now Granny was ill he was more determined to do it than ever.

He had until tea time to plan the

greatest
jewel theft
in history.

19

A SMALL EXPLOSIVE DEVICE

The next morning, as Mum and Dad went through song after song to select some music for their son's upcoming dance competition, Ben sneaked out of the house and cycled to the hospital.

When he finally found Granny's ward, he saw that there was a bespectacled doctor perched on her bed. Nevertheless, he raced over excitedly to see the old lady, so he could share the plan with her.

The doctor was holding Granny's hand and talking to her slowly and quietly.

"Just give us a moment alone, please, Ben," said Granny. "The doctor and I are just talking about, you know, lady things."

"Oh, er, OK," said Ben. He sloped back to the swing doors, and leafed through a sickly-looking copy of *Take a Break*.

The doctor passed him and said, "I'm sorry," before leaving the ward.

Sorry? thought Ben. *Why is he sorry?*

And he walked **tentatively** over to his granny's bed.

Granny was dabbing at her eyes with a tissue, but when she saw Ben approach she stopped and shoved it back up the sleeve of her nightdress.

"Are you OK, Granny?" he asked softly.

"Yes, I'm fine. I just have something in my eye."

"Then why did the doctor say 'I'm sorry' to me?"

Granny looked flustered for a moment.

"Erm, well, I imagine he was sorry that he wasted your time in coming here. There is absolutely nothing wrong with me, as it turns out."

"Really?"

"Yes, the doctor gave me the test results. I'm as fit as a butcher's dog."

Ben hadn't heard that expression before, but he imagined it must mean very, very fit.

"That's brilliant news, Granny," exclaimed Ben. "Now, I know you said 'no' before—"

"Is this what I think it is, Ben?" asked Granny.

Ben nodded.

"I said 'no' a hundred times."

"Yes, but—"

"But what, young man?"

"I've found a weakness in the Tower of London. And I have spent all week working on a plan of how we can steal the jewels. I think we can really do it."

To his surprise, Granny looked intrigued. "Pull the curtains and keep your voice down," hissed the old lady, flicking the switch on her hearing aid to full power.

Ben quickly pulled the curtains round Granny's bed, and then sat down next to her.

"So, at the stroke of midnight we swim across the Thames in scuba-diving gear, and locate the ancient sewage pipe, here," whispered Ben, showing her the detailed diagram in the back issue of **PLUMBING WEEKLY**.

"We have to swim up a sewage pipe?! At my age!" said Granny. "Don't be daft, boy!"

"Shush, keep your voice down," said Ben.

"Sorry," whispered Granny.

"And it's not daft. It's brilliant. The pipe is just wide enough, look here…"

Granny lifted herself up from her pillows and moved closer to the page in **PLUMBING WEEKLY**. She studied the diagram. It did indeed look wide enough.

"Now, if we swim up the pipe we can get inside the Tower undetected," continued Ben. "Everywhere else around the perimeter of the building there are armed guards and security cameras and laser sensors. Take any other route in and we wouldn't stand a chance."

"Yes, yes, yes, but then how the blazes do we get into the Jewel House where the jewels are kept?" she whispered.

"The sewage pipe ends here at the privy."

"I beg your pardon?"

"The privy. It's an old word for toilet."

"Oh yes, so it is."

"From the privy it's a short run—"

"Ahem!"

"Er, I mean a short **walk** across the courtyard to the Jewel House. At night the door to the house is of course **locked** and **double locked**."

"Probably **triple locked!**" Granny didn't

seem that convinced. Well, Ben would just have to convince her!

"The door is solid steel, so we'll drill out the locks to open it—"

"But the crowns and the sceptres and all that gubbins must surely be kept behind bulletproof glass, Ben," said Granny.

"Yes, but the glass isn't bombproof. We'll set off a small explosive device to shatter the glass."

"An **explosive** device?!" spluttered Granny. "Where on earth are we going to get that from?"

"I swiped a few chemicals from Science class," replied Ben with a smirk. "I am pretty sure I can create an explosion big enough to get through that glass."

"But the guards will hear the explosion, Ben. No, no, no. I'm sorry, that's never going to work!" exclaimed Granny as quietly as she could.

"Well, I thought of that," said Ben, momentarily delighted with his own ingenuity. "You need to board a train to London earlier that day, posing as a sweet old lady —"

"I *am* a sweet old lady!" protested Granny.

"You know what I mean," continued Ben with a smile. "From the station you take the number seventy-eight bus, all the way to the Tower of London. Then you give the Beefeater guards chocolate cake with something in it to make them sleep."

"Oh, I could use my **special herbal sleeping tonic!**" said Granny.

"Er, yes, fantastic," said Ben. "So, the guards eat the chocolate cake, and by night-time they will be fast asleep."

"Chocolate cake?" protested Granny. "Surely the guards would prefer some of my delicious home-made **cabbage** cake*."

* Granny's recipe for CABBAGE CAKE:

Take six large mouldy cabbages

Mash up the cabbages with your

potato masher

Put the cabbage mush into a baking tray

Bake in the oven until your whole house

smells of cabbage

Wait a month for the cake to go stale

Slice and serve (sick bucket optional)

"Erm," Ben squirmed.

He didn't want to upset Granny, but there was no way anyone would eat a piece of Granny's cabbage cake unless they were intimately related to her, and even then they would probably spit it out when she wasn't looking.

"I think a chocolate cake from the supermarket would be better."

"Well, you seem to have thought of everything. I'm very impressed, you know. The idea of using that old pipe is **GENIUS.**"

Ben flushed with pride. "Thanks."

"But how did you know about it? They don't teach you that stuff at school do they, about sewage pipes and that?"

"No," said Ben. "It's just... I've always loved plumbing. I remembered the old pipes being in my favourite magazine." He held up **PLUMBING WEEKLY.** "It's my dream to be a plumber one day."

He looked down, expecting Granny to tell him off or mock him.

"Why are you looking at the ground?" asked Granny.

"Um… Well, I know it's silly and boring to want to be a plumber. I know I should want to do something more interesting." Ben felt his face turn burning red.

Granny put a hand on his chin and gently tilted his head up. "Nothing you do could ever be silly or boring, Ben," she said. "If you want to be a plumber, and it's your dream, then no one can take it away from you. Do you understand? All you can do in this life is follow your dreams. Otherwise you're just wasting your time."

"I… I guess."

"I should hope so. Honestly! You say that plumbing is boring, but here you are, planning to steal the *Crown Jewels*, for goodness' sake… and it's all down to plumbing!"

Ben smiled. Maybe Granny was right.

"But I have a question for you, Ben."

"Yes?"

"How do we escape? A plan like this is no good if you are going to get caught red-handed, my lad."

"I know that, Granny, so I thought we should go out the way we came in, through the sewage pipe, and swim back across the Thames. It's only fifty metres wide, and I've got my hundred-metre swimming badge. It will be a doddle."

Granny bit her lip. She obviously wasn't sure that any of this would be a doddle, not least swimming across a fast-flowing river at night.

Ben looked at her with hope in his eyes.

"Well, Granny, are you in? Are you still a gangsta?"

She looked deep in thought for quite a while.

"Please?" pleaded Ben. "I've loved hearing all about your adventures, and I really want to go on a heist with you. And this would be the ultimate: stealing the *Crown Jewels*. You said yourself it was every great thief's dream. Well, Granny? Are you in?"

Granny looked at her grandson's glowing face. After a while she murmured, "Yes."

Ben leaped from his chair and hugged her.

"Brilliant!"

Granny lifted her weak arms and embraced him. It was the first time in years she had really hugged him.

"But I have one condition," said the old lady with a deadly serious look in her eyes.

"What?" whispered Ben.

"We put them back the next night."

20

Ben couldn't believe what Granny had just said. There was no way he would risk stealing the *Crown Jewels* only to put them back the very next night.

"But they are worth millions, billions even…" he complained.

"I know. So we'd definitely get caught if we tried to sell them," replied Granny.

"But…!"

"No 'buts', boy. We put them back the next night. Do you know how I evaded prison all these years? I never sold a thing. I just did it for the buzz."

"But you kept them, though," said Ben. "Even if you didn't sell them. You've got all those jewels in your biscuit tin."

Granny blinked. "Yes, well, I was young and foolish then," she said. "I have learned since that it is wrong to steal. And you need to understand that too." She gave him a fierce look.

Ben squirmed. "I do, of course I do…"

"It's a brilliant plan you've put together, Ben, honestly it is. But those jewels don't belong to us, do they?"

"No," said Ben. "No, they don't." He felt a tiny bit ashamed now that he'd been so horrified at the idea of giving back the jewels.

"And don't forget that every policeman in the country, maybe even the world, will be looking for the *Crown Jewels*. They'll have all of Scotland Yard after us. If we were found with them we'd be thrown into prison for the rest of our lives. That might not be so long for me, but for you it could be seventy or eighty years."

"You're right," said Ben.

"And the Queen seems like such a nice old dear. We are around the same age actually. I would hate to upset her."

"Me too," murmured Ben. He had seen the Queen on the news loads of times and she seemed like a nice old lady, smiling and waving at everybody from the back of her giant pram.

"Let's just do it for the **THRILL.** Agreed?"

"Agreed!" said Ben. "When can we do it? It will have to be a Friday night when Mum and Dad take me to stay at yours. Did the doctor say when you'll be out of hospital?"

"Erm, oh yes, he did, he said I could leave any time."

"Fantastic!"

"But we need to do it very soon. How about next Friday?"

"Isn't that too soon?"

"Not at all, your plan seems very well-thought-out, Ben."

"Thank you," said Ben, beaming. It was the first time ever that he felt like he had made a grown-up proud of him.

"When I get out of here I'll get on to pinching the equipment we need. Now run along, Ben, and I will see you next Friday night at the usual time."

Ben pulled back the curtain. Mr Parker, Granny's nosy neighbour, was standing right there!

Startled, Ben took a couple of steps back towards the bed, and quickly shoved **PLUMBING WEEKLY** up the back of his jumper.

"What are *you* doing here?" asked Ben.

"Hoping to see me take a bed bath, no doubt!" said Granny.

Ben chuckled.

Mr Parker scrambled for words. "No, no, I…"

"Matron! MATRON!" hollered Granny.

"Wait!" said Mr Parker, panicking. "I'm sure I heard one of you talking about the *Crown Jewels*…"

It was too late. The matron, who was an unusually tall lady with very big feet, **clomped** down the ward at speed.

"Yes?" asked the matron. "Is something the matter?"

"This man was **spying** on me through the curtains!" said Granny.

"Were you?" demanded Matron, eyeballing Mr Parker.

"Well, er, I heard that they were…" whined Mr Parker.

"Last week he spied on my granny doing her naked yoga," offered Ben.

Matron's face turned puce with **HORROR**. "Get out of my ward at once, you filthy little swine!" she screamed.

Humiliated, Mr Parker backed away from the terrifying matron and scuttled out of the ward. He paused at the swing doors and yelled back to Granny and Ben, "YOU HAVEN'T SEEN THE LAST OF ME!" before rushing out.

"Please let me know if that man comes back," said Matron, her face returning to a more normal shade.

"I will," replied Granny, before Matron returned to her duties.

"He could have heard everything!" hissed Ben.

"Maybe," replied Granny. "But I think Matron scared him off for good!"

"I hope so." Ben was very worried about this unfortunate development.

"Do you still want to go through with it?" asked the old lady.

Ben had that feeling you have when you are on a rollercoaster and it's slowly making its way UP the track. You want to get off and you want to stay on. Dread and delight all rolled into one.

"Yes!" he said.

"Hurrah!" said Granny, giving Ben a big smile.

Ben turned to leave, then turned round. "I… I love you, Granny," he said.

"And I love you too, little Benny," said Granny with a wink.

Ben winced. He had a **gangsta granny** now, and that was great – but he was going to have to teach her to just call him Ben!

*

Ben ran along the corridors, his heart beating incredibly fast.

BOOM BOOM BOOM.

He was electrified with excitement. This eleven-year-old boy, who had never done anything notable in his life except once been sick on his friend's head on the big wheel at the local funfair, was going to take part in the most daring robbery the world has ever known.

He ran outside the hospital, and began fumbling with the keys to unlock his bike from the railing. Then, looking up, he saw something unbelievable.

It was his granny.

That, in itself, was not unusual.

But this was:

Granny was abseiling down the side of the hospital.

She had tied a number of bed sheets together and was lowering herself at speed down the side of the building.

Ben couldn't believe his eyes. He knew his granny was a proper gangsta, but this was off the scale!

"Granny, what on earth are you doing?!" shouted Ben across the car park.

"The lift wasn't working, dear! See you next Friday. Don't be late!" she shouted as she reached the ground, leaped on her mobility scooter and roared off... well, **whirred** off home.

*

Never had a week passed so slowly.

Ben spent all week waiting for Friday to come. Every minute, every hour, every day seemed like an eternity.

It was strange having to pretend he was just another ordinary boy when really he was one of the greatest criminal masterminds of all time.

Finally, Friday evening came. There was a knock on Ben's bedroom door.

RAT-TAT-TAT.

"Well, are you ready, son?" said Dad.

"Yeah," said Ben, trying to act as innocent as possible, which is actually quite hard when you are feeling extremely guilty. "You don't need to pick me up too early in the morning tomorrow – Granny and I normally play SCRABBLE until quite late."

"You won't be playing SCRABBLE, son," said Dad.

"No?"

"No, son. You won't be going to Granny's tonight at all."

"Oh no!" said Ben. "Is she back in hospital?"

"No, she's not."

Ben sighed with relief then felt a prickle of anxiety. "So, why am I not going to her house?"

The plan was in place, and there was no time to lose!

"Because," said Dad, "tonight it's the under-twelve dancing championships. At last it's your big moment to shine!"

21

A TAP-SHOE

Ben sat silently in the back of the little brown car in his **Love Bomb** outfit.

"I hope you didn't forget about the competition, Ben," said Mum, as she fixed her make-up in the passenger seat, her lipstick accidentally scrawling across her face as they went round a corner.

"No, of course not, Mum."

"Don't worry, son," continued Dad, as he proudly drove his son to dance-competition immortality. "You've done so much training up in your bedroom, I know you'll get top marks from all the judges. Straight tens!"

"What about Granny? Won't she be expecting me?" said Ben anxiously.

Tonight was supposed to be the night that they stole the *Crown Jewels*, but instead he was on his way to take part in a dance competition, despite never having danced a step in his life.

For the last two weeks, he had avoided thinking about the dance competition, but now the time had come.

It was really going to happen.

He was going to have to dance a solo number.

Which he hadn't prepared.

In front of an entire theatre full of people…

"Oh, don't worry about Granny," said Mum. "She doesn't know what day it is!" She laughed, as the car stopped suddenly at a red light and mascara **splattered** over her forehead.

They arrived at the town hall. Ben saw a

rushing river of multicoloured Lycra making its way into the building.

If anyone at school found out he'd entered, he would never live this down. The bullies would have all the ammunition they would need to make his life hell **for ever.** And what's more, he hadn't rehearsed his dance. Not even once. He didn't have a clue what he was going to do on stage.

This was a competition to find the best junior dancers in the local area. There was a prize for best couple, best solo female and best solo male.

If you won here, you would get the chance to compete for your county, and if you won there, for your country.

This was the first step on the road to international dance superstardom. And the host for the evening was none other than **STRICTLY STARS DANCING** heartthrob and his mum's favourite, **Flavio Flavioli.**

"It's wonderful to see so many beautiful ladies here tonight," he purred in his Italian accent.

Flavio looked even more shiny in real life. His hair was slicked back, his teeth were dazzlingly white and his outfit was as tight as clingfilm. *"Now, are we all ready to rumba?"*

The crowd all screamed, "Yes!"

*"***Flavio** *can't hear you. I said, 'Are you ready to rumba?'"*

"YES!" they all screamed again, a little louder than before.

Ben was listening nervously backstage. He heard one woman's voice screech, "I love you, **Flavio!**" It sounded suspiciously like his mum.

Ben looked around the dressing room. It might as well have been a convention of the most annoying children in the world. They looked so unbearably **precocious,** adorned in these ridiculously garish Lycra outfits, smeared in fake tan, and with pearly white teeth so bright they could be seen from outer space.

Ben looked anxiously at his watch, knowing he was going to be terribly late to meet his granny. He waited and waited as the over-made-up quickstepped, jived, waltzed, Viennese waltzed, tangoed, foxtrotted and cha-cha-cha-ed.

Finally, Ben's turn came. He stood in the wings as **Flavio** announced him.

"Now it's time for a local boy who is going to delight us all tonight with a solo dance piece. Please welcome Ben!"

Flavio glided off the stage as Ben plodded on, his Lycra LOVE BOMB outfit riding uncomfortably up his bottom.

Ben stood alone in the middle of the dance floor. A spotlight shone on him. The music started up. He was praying for some sort of escape from this. He would have been happy with anything at all, including:

A fire alarm

An earthquake

World War III

Another Ice Age

A deadly swarm of killer bees

A meteor from outer space hitting the earth and spinning it off its axis

A tidal wave

Flavio Flavioli being attacked by hundreds of flesh-eating zombies

A hurricane or tornado (Ben didn't really know the difference, but either would do)

Ben being abducted by aliens, and not returning to the earth for a thousand years

Dinosaurs returning to the earth through some

kind of time/space portal, and smashing through the roof before devouring everyone inside

A volcano erupting, though annoyingly there didn't seem to be any volcanoes nearby

An attack of giant slugs

Even an attack of medium-sized slugs would do.

Ben wasn't fussy. Any of the above would have sufficed.

The music played for a while and Ben realised he hadn't moved his body yet. He looked over at his parents, who beamed with pride at seeing their only child **centre stage** at last.

He looked to the wings where the ever-smiling **Flavio** was giving him an encouraging grin.

Please, make the ground open up now...

It didn't.

There was no choice but to do something. Anything.

Ben started moving his legs, then his arms, then his head. None of these parts of his body moved in time or sequence, and for the next five minutes he threw his body around the dance floor in a style that can only be called **unforgettable:** as much as you might want to forget it, you can't.

Ben tried a jump at the end, just as the music stopped, and he fell to the floor with a **THUD.** There was SILENCE. DEAFENING SILENCE.

Then Ben could hear the sound of one pair of hands clapping. He looked up.

It was his mum.

Then another pair of hands joined in.

It was his dad.

For a few seconds he thought it might be one of those moments you see in a film when the underdog triumphs against all the odds: that soon everyone in the hall would be on their feet cheering and applauding this local boy who had at last made his loved ones proud and at the same time re-invented dancing for ever.

THE END.

Well, no. That's not what happened.

After a few moments, his parents felt embarrassed to be the only people applauding, and stopped.

Flavio returned to the stage.

"Well, that was, that was..." For the first time

the Italian heartthrob seemed lost for words. *"Judges, can we have your scores for Ben, please?"*

"Zero," said the first.

"Zero."

"Zero."

Only one more judge to go. Could Ben make it four zeros?

But the final judge must have felt sorry for the sweaty little boy in front of her who had shamed his family for generations to come with his epic display of talentlessness. She shuffled her scoring paddles under the desk. "One," she announced.

There were loud boos and jeers from the audience so she corrected her score. "I am sorry, I mean zero," she said, holding up her original choice of paddle.

"Slightly disappointing scores from the judges, there," said **Flavio**, still trying hard to smile.

"But, young Ben, all is not lost. As the only boy who entered the solo male category tonight, you are therefore the winner. May I present you with this solid plastic statuette."

Flavio picked up a cheap-looking trophy of a dancing boy, and presented it to Ben.

"Ladies and gentlemen, boys and girls, a round of applause for Ben!"

There was silence again. Even Mum and Dad didn't dare to clap.

Then boos started, and then jeers and catcalls: shouts of "SHAME ON YOU!" "NO!" and "FIX!"

Flavio's perfect smile began to **crack.** He leaned down to Ben and whispered in his ear, *"You'd better get out of here before you get lynched."*

At that exact moment a tap-shoe was thrown from the back of the audience. It flew at speed through the air. It was probably aimed at Ben,

but instead it hit **Flavio** right between the eyes, and he fell to the ground u n c o n s c i o u s.

Time to make my excuses and leave, thought Ben.

22

LYCRA LYNCH MOB

An angry mob of **ballroom-dancing** enthusiasts chased the little brown car down the street. Looking out of the back window, Ben thought this would perhaps be the only time in history a lynch mob was dressed entirely in Lycra.

Dad put his foot down on the accelerator

VVVVVVVRRRRRRRRR RRRROOOOOOOOO OOOOMMMMMMMM MMM!

...and they turned a corner and lost them.

"Thank goodness I was there to give **Flavio** the kiss of life!" said Mum from the fron t seat.

"He was just unconscious. He hadn't stopped breathing, Mum," said Ben from the back.

"You can't be too careful," said Mum, re-applying her lipstick. Most of it was now smeared over **Flavio's** face and neck.

"Your performance was, in a word, dreadful and embarrassing," pronounced Dad.

"That's two words," corrected Ben with a chuckle. "Three if you count the 'and'."

"Don't get funny with me, young lad," snapped Dad. "This is no laughing matter. I was ashamed of you. Ashamed."

"Yes, ashamed," grumbled Mum in agreement.

Ben felt like he would give anything to disappear. He would give all of his past and all of his future, just so he didn't have to be sitting in the back seat of his mum and dad's car right now.

"I'm sorry, Mum," said Ben. "I want to make you proud, I really do." It was true: making his parents ashamed, well, that was the absolute last thing he wanted, however stupid he thought they were sometimes.

"Well, you have a funny way of showing it," said Mum.

"I just don't like dancing, that's all."

"That's not the point. Your mother spent hours making your costume," said Dad.

It's strange how parents always refer to each other as "Mother" or "Father" rather than "Mum" or "Dad" when you are in trouble.

"You made no effort up there on the stage whatsoever," Dad continued. "I don't think you even rehearsed once. Not once. Me and your mother work night and day to give you the opportunities we never had, and this is how you treat us…"

"With contempt," said Mum.

"Contempt," echoed Dad.

A single tear ran down Ben's cheek. He caught it with his tongue. It tasted bitter. The three sat in silence as the car rumbled home.

No words were spoken as they got out of the car, and went into the house. As soon as Dad opened the front door, Ben bounded up to his room and slammed the door. He sat on his bed, still in his **LOVE BOMB** outfit.

Ben had never felt more alone. He was hours late to meet Granny. Not only had he let down his mum and dad, he had let down the one person he had grown to love more than anyone – his granny.

They were never going to steal the *Crown Jewels* now.

Just at that moment, there was a quiet **tap** on his window.

It was Granny.

Dressed in her scuba-diving gear the old lady had climbed a ladder to reach her grandson's bedroom window.

"Let me in!" she mouthed theatrically.

Ben couldn't help but smile. He opened the window and hauled the old lady inside, like a fisherman might haul a particularly big fish on to his boat.

"You are very late," admonished Granny as Ben helped her over to the bed.

"I know, I'm sorry," said Ben.

"We said seven o'clock. It's half past ten. The sleeping tonic I gave the guards at the Tower will be wearing off soon. "

"I'm really sorry. It's a long story," said Ben.

Granny sat on Ben's bed and looked him up

and down. "And why are you dressed like a demented **VALENTINE'S CARD?**" she demanded.

"As I said, it's a long story…"

It was a bit rich for Granny to criticise what he had on considering she was dressed in a wetsuit and scuba-diving mask, but there wasn't time to get into that now.

"Quick, boy, put on this wetsuit, and follow me down the ladder. I'll start up the mobility scooter."

"Are we really going to steal the *Crown Jewels*, Granny?"

"Well, we are going to have a go!" said the old lady with a smile.

23

CAUGHT
BY THE
FUZZ

They whirred through the town: Granny driving, Ben clinging on behind her. Both in wetsuits and diving masks, with Granny's handbag wrapped in miles of clingfilm sitting in the basket at the front.

Granny spotted Raj closing up his newsagent's shop.

"Hello, Raj, dear, don't forget to save me some **Murray Mints** for Monday!" she shouted.

Raj looked at the two of them, open-mouthed in shock.

"I don't know what's got into him. He's

normally so chatty!"

It was a long way to London, especially on a motorised scooter with a top speed of three miles per hour (with two passengers).

After a while Ben noticed the roads getting

wider and wider; two lanes, then three lanes.

"Bums! We are on the motorway!" shouted
Ben from the back as ten-ton lorries *whooshed*
past, nearly wrenching the scooter off the road
with the force of their slipstream.

"You know, you really shouldn't swear, young man," said Granny. "Now, I'm going to step on it so hold on **tight!**"

A moment later, a particularly big petrol tanker thundered by, inches from their heads, beeping its horn.

"Big hairy bums!" said Granny.

"Granny!" said Ben, shocked.

"Whoops, that one just slipped out!" said Granny. Grown-ups *never* lead by example.

"I'm sorry, Granny, but I am not sure this thing is built for a motorway," said Ben. Just then an even bigger lorry blustered past. Ben could feel the wheels of the scooter **lift off** the road for a second, as the slipstream dragged it in the lorry's wake.

"I'll take the next exit," said Granny. But before she could, flashing blue lights began to spin behind them. "Oh no, it's the fuzz! Let's see if I can outrun them." She **SLAMMED** her foot on the accelerator, and the scooter leaped from three miles per hour to three and a half miles per hour.

The police car drove alongside them, and the officer inside gestured angrily for them to pull over.

"Granny, you'd better pull over," said Ben. "We're done for."

"Let me handle this, my boy."

Granny stopped the mobility scooter on the hard shoulder as the police car parked in front of them, blocking any chance of escape.

"Is this your vehicle, Madam?" said the police officer. He was big and had a small moustache, which made his round face look even rounder. He also had a smug expression on his face that suggested telling people off was his favourite thing in the world. His name tag said that he was called PC Fudge.

"Is there a problem, Officer?" said Granny innocently, her diving mask a little steamed up from all the excitement.

"Yes, there is a problem. The use of motorised mobility scooters on motorways is strictly prohibited," said the police officer in a patronising tone.

(Other modes of transport not permitted on a motorway are:

Skateboard

Canoe

Roller skates

Donkey

Shopping trolley

Unicycle

Sledge

Rickshaw

Camel

Magic carpet

Comedy ostrich.)

"Well, thank you so much for pointing that out, Officer. We'll remember for next time. Now if you'll excuse us we are running a little late. Goodbye!" said Granny cheerily, as she restarted the mobility scooter.

"Have you been drinking, Madam?"

"I had some cabbage soup before I came out."

"Alcohol, I mean," he sighed.

"I had a brandy liqueur chocolate on Tuesday night. Does that count?"

Ben couldn't help but chuckle.

PC Fudge's eyes narrowed. "Then would you care to explain to me why you are dressed in scuba-diving gear with your handbag wrapped in clingfilm?"

This was going to take some explaining.

"Because, because, erm…" Granny was stumbling over her words.

They were done for.

"Because we are from the **CLINGFILM APPRECIATION SOCIETY,**" said Ben with authority.

"I've never heard of that!" said PC Fudge dismissively.

"We are very new," said Ben.

"Just two members so far," added Granny, continuing the lie. "And we like to keep the society low-key, so we have our meetings underwater, hence the wetsuits."

The policeman looked utterly **baffled.** Granny didn't stop talking, apparently in the hope that she might baffle him further.

"Now, if you'll excuse us, we are in rather a hurry. We have to get to London for an important meeting with the BUBBLE WRAP APPRECIATION SOCIETY. We are thinking of merging the two organisations."

PC Fudge was all but lost for words. "How many members have they got?"

"Just one," said Granny. "But if we join forces we can save money on teabags and photocopying and paperclips and the like. Goodbye!"

Granny put her foot down on the accelerator and the mobility scooter *lurched* off.

"STOP RIGHT THERE!" said PC Fudge, holding his hand out straight in front of him.

Ben froze in terror. He wasn't even twelve yet, and he was going to spend the rest of his life in jail.

PC Fudge leaned over and put his face next to Granny's.

"I'll give you a lift."

24

DARK WATERS

"Just here, please," said Granny, directing from the back seat of the police car. "Just opposite the Tower. Thank you so much."

PC Fudge strained as he unloaded the scooter out of his boot. "Well, next time, please remember that mobility scooters are meant only for pavements, not main roads, and certainly not motorways."

"Yes, Officer," replied Granny with a smile.

"Well, good luck you two, with the whole… erm… clingfilm-bubble wrap alliance thing."

And with that, PC Fudge sped off into

the night, leaving Granny and Ben gazing at the magnificent thousand-year-old Tower of London on the opposite bank of the river. It was particularly **spectacular** at night, its four domed towers lit up, its reflection shimmering on the cold dark River Thames below.

The Tower was once a prison, with an illustrious list of former inmates (including the future Queen Elizabeth I, the adventurer Sir Walter Raleigh, the terrorist Guy Fawkes, the senior Nazi Rudolf Hess, and my mother*). Now, though, the Tower is a museum, and home to the priceless *Crown Jewels*, housed in their own special building, the Jewel House.

* I lied about that last one: my mother was never locked up in the Tower of London. But she should be because she puts coffee in banoffee pie. She says the "offee" in "banoffee" is for coffee when actually it should be toffee.

The unlikely pair of gangstas stood on the riverbank. "Are you ready?" asked Granny, her mask completely steamed up from sitting in the back of a police car for over an hour.

"Yes," said Ben, trembling with excitement. "I'm ready."

Granny reached out to hold Ben's hand, and then she counted, "Three, two, one," and on "one" they leaped into the dark waters below.

The water was **FREEZING** cold even with the wetsuits on, and for a few moments all Ben

could see was black. It was **TERRIFYING** and **exhilarating** in equal measure.

When their heads bobbed out of the water, Ben took the snorkel out of his mouth for a moment.

"Are you OK, Granny?"

"I have never felt more alive."

They doggy-paddled across the river. Ben had never been a great swimmer and lagged behind a little. Secretly he wished he had brought his armbands or at least a Lilo.

A huge party cruiser, with music blaring and young people shouting, chugged down the river. Granny had swum ahead, and Ben had lost sight of her.

Oh no!

Had she been **crushed** by the cruiser?

Was Granny in a watery grave at the bottom of the Thames?

"Come on, slowcoach!" shouted Granny as the party boat passed and they caught sight of each other again. Ben sighed with relief, and continued doggy-paddling across the deep dark dirty water.

According to the diagram in **PLUMBING WEEKLY**, the sewage pipe was situated just to the left of TRAITORS' GATE. (This was an entrance to the Tower only accessible from the river, where many prisoners would be taken to be locked up for the rest of their lives or beheaded. Nowadays TRAITORS' GATE had been bricked up, so the pipe was the only way into the Tower from the river.)

Then, with a rush of relief, Ben found the pipe. It was partly submerged under the water. It was **dark** and **eerie,** and he could hear the echoes of lapping waves reverberating inside it.

Suddenly Ben began to have second thoughts about the whole adventure. As much as he liked plumbing, he didn't want to have to crawl up an ancient sewage pipe.

"Come on, Ben," said Granny, as she bobbed up and down in the water. "We haven't come this far to give up now."

Well, thought Ben. *If a little old lady can do it, then I certainly can.*

Ben took a deep breath and propelled himself into the pipe. Granny followed close behind.

It was blacker than black in there, and after he'd travelled a few metres he could feel something crawling across his head. He heard an EEK-EEK noise, and could sense something scratching his scalp.

It felt like claws.

He put his hand on his head.

He touched something big and furry.

Then he realised the awful truth.

IT WAS A RAT!

A giant rat was clinging to the top of his head.

"AAAAHHHHHHHHH!"

screamed Ben.

25

The sound of Ben's scream echoed through the length of the pipe. He **WHACKED** the rat off his head and it landed on top of Granny, who was crawling up the pipe just behind him.

"Poor little rat," she said. "Be gentle with it, dear."

"But—"

"It was here first. Now come on, we have to hurry. The sleeping-tonic chocolate cake I gave the guards will be wearing off very soon."

The pair crawled further up the pipe. It was wet and slippery, and it smelled awful.

(Unfortunately for Ben and Granny, it turns out that ancient poo does still pong.)

After a while, Ben could see a shaft of grey in all the black. It was the end of the tunnel, at last!

He hauled himself out of the ancient stone privy, and then reached down the pipe to help his granny clamber out. They were COVERED from head to toe in disgustingly stinky black slime.

Standing inside the cold dark toilet, Ben spied a glassless window in the wall. They clambered through this and landed on the cold, wet grass of the Tower's courtyard below.

For a few moments they lay there, gazing up at the moon and the stars. Ben reached out and held Granny's hand. She squeezed it tight.

"This is amazing," said Ben.

"Come on, dear," she whispered. "We've barely started yet!"

Ben stood up and helped Granny to her feet.

The old lady immediately started unwrapping the clingfilm that she had waterproofed her handbag with.

This took several minutes.

"I think I may have overdone the clingfilm. Still, better safe than sorry."

Eventually the mile-long roll of clingfilm was off, and Granny took out a map Ben had cut out of a book in the school library, so the two unlikely thieves could locate the Jewel House.

It was **eerie** being inside the Tower of London courtyard at night.

The Tower is said to be haunted by the ghosts of people who died there. Over the years, several guards have run away in terror, claiming that at the dead of night they had seen the ghosts of various historical figures who had died there.

Now, though, there was something even

stranger roaming the courtyard.

Granny in a wetsuit!

"This way," hissed Granny, and Ben followed her down a walled passage. Ben's heart was beating so fast he thought he was going to **explode.**

After a few minutes they were standing outside the Jewel House, overlooking Tower Green and the monument to those who were beheaded or hanged there. Ben wondered if he and Granny would be executed if they were caught stealing the *Crown Jewels,* and a shiver ran down his spine.

Two Beefeaters were lying on the ground, snoring loudly. Their immaculate black-and-red uniforms emblazoned with "ER" were becoming soiled on the wet ground. Granny's herbal sleeping tonic in the chocolate cake had worked.

But for how long?

As she hurried past them, Granny let out a familiar quacking sound from her bum. One of the guards' noses crinkled at the smell.

Ben held his breath – not just because of the smell – but because he was afraid.

Was Granny's bottom burp going to wake the guard up and ruin everything?

An eternal moment passed…

Then the guard opened one eye.

Oh no!

Granny pushed Ben back, and raised her handbag, as if to clobber the Beefeater with it.

This is it, thought Ben. *We'll be* **hanged!**

But then the guard closed his eye again, and continued snoring.

"Granny, please try to control your bottom," hissed Ben.

"I didn't do a thing," said Granny innocently. "It must have been you."

They tiptoed to the huge steel door at the front of the Jewel House.

"Right, I just need your dad's power drill…"

said Granny, reaching inside her handbag. With a juddering *WHIRR,* she started drilling through the series of locks on the door. One by one the metal locks crumbled to the ground.

All of a sudden the guards snored extremely loudly.

ZZZZZZZZZZZZZZZZZZzz
zzZZZZzzzzzzZZZZzzzzzZZ
zzzzzZZZZZZZzzzzzzzzZZZ!

Ben froze and Granny nearly dropped the power drill. But the guards slept on and, after a few nerve-racking minutes, the door was finally unlocked.

Granny looked exhausted. Sweat was dripping down her forehead. She sat down on a low wall for a moment, and then pulled out a Thermos flask.

"Cabbage soup?" she offered.

"No, thank you, Granny," replied Ben. He shifted uneasily. "We'd better get going before the guards wake up."

"Rush, rush, rush, that's all you kids do these days. Patience is a virtue." She poured the last of her cabbage soup down her throat, and rose to her feet.

"Delicious! Right, let's do this!" she said.

The huge steel door creaked as it opened, and Ben and Granny entered the Jewel House.

Out of the dark, came a flurry of black feathers, hitting Ben and Granny in the face. Ben was so startled he screamed again.

"Shush!" said Granny.

"What were they?" said Ben, as he saw the winged creatures disappear off into the black sky. "Bats?"

"No, dear – ravens. There are dozens of

them here. Ravens have lived at the Tower for hundreds of years."

"This place is **spooky,**" said Ben, his stomach knotted in fear.

"Especially at night," agreed Granny. "Now stay close to me, boy, because it's about to get a whole lot **spookier...**"

26

A long winding corridor stretched out ahead of them. This was where tourists from around the world queued for hours to see the *Crown Jewels*. The old lady and her grandson tiptoed their way silently along it, dripping smelly icy water from the Thames in their wake.

Finally they turned a corner, into the main room where all the jewels were kept. Like the sun bursting through the clouds on a grey day, the jewels illuminated Ben and Granny's faces.

The pair of thieves stopped in awe. Their mouths fell open as they looked at the treasures laid out before them. They were more magnificent than anyone could imagine. It truly was the most superb collection of precious objects in the world.

Dear reader, not only are they beautiful and priceless, they symbolise hundreds of years of history. There are a number of royal crowns:

- St Edward's Crown, with which the new king or queen is crowned by the Archbishop of Canterbury during the coronation ceremony. It's made of gold and decorated with sapphires and topazes. PROPER BLING!
- The Imperial State Crown, in which are set an incredible three thousand gems, including the Second Star of Africa (the second-largest stone cut from the largest diamond ever found. No, I don't know where the First Star is).

- The breathtaking Imperial Crown of India, set with around six thousand diamonds and magnificent rubies and emeralds. Unfortunately not in my size.

- The twelfth-century gold Anointing Spoon, used to anoint the king or queen with holy oil. Not to be used for eating **Coco Pops.**

- Not forgetting the Ampulla, the gold flask in the form of an eagle that contains that holy oil. Like a really posh Thermos flask.

- And finally, the famous Orb and Sceptres. That's a lot of gear.

If the *Crown Jewels* were featured in the Argos catalogue, they would probably look like this:

Granny took out the rolled-up supermarket carrier bag she'd kept in her handbag, ready to put the *Crown Jewels* in. "Right, we just need to break through this glass," she whispered.

Ben looked at her with disbelief. "I'm not sure we are going to get all of these jewels in there."

"Well, sorry, dear," she whispered back. "You have to pay five pence for plastic bags at the shops these days, so I only bought the one."

The glass was inches thick.

Bulletproof.

Ben had smuggled a few compound chemicals out of his Science class, and combined them to go…

KKKKKKKAAAAAAAAAAA BBBBBBBBBOOOOOOOOOO MMMMMMMMMM!!!!!!!!!!!!!!!!!!!!

…if set alight.

They stuck the chemicals to the glass with some

BluTack. Then Granny attached one end of a ball of pink wool to the BluTack. (Wool would be the perfect fuse.) Then she produced some matches. They just needed to make sure they were far enough away from the explosion. Otherwise they might be blown up too.

"Right, Ben," whispered Granny. "Let's get as far away from the glass as we can."

The pair retreated round a wall, unravelling the pink wool as they went.

"Do you want to light the fuse?" said Granny.

Ben nodded. He really wanted to, but his hands were trembling so much with excitement he didn't know if he could.

Ben opened the matchbox. There were only two matches inside.

He went to strike the first, but his hands were shaking so much that it broke in two when he did.

"Oh dear," whispered Granny. "Have another go."

Ben picked up the second match.

He tried to strike it but nothing happened. Some river water must have leaked out of the sleeve of his wetsuit. Now both the match and the matchbox were soaking wet.

"**Noooo!**" cried Ben in desperation. "Mum and Dad were right. I am useless. I can't even light a match!"

Granny put her arms round her grandson.

As they cuddled, their wetsuits *squeaked* a little.

"Don't talk like that, Ben. You are an amazing young man. You really are. Since we have been spending so much time together I am a hundred times happier than I could ever say."

"Really?" said Ben.

"Really!" replied Granny. "And you are

so very clever. You planned this whole extraordinary heist yourself and you're only eleven years old."

"I'm nearly twelve," said Ben.

Granny chuckled. "But you get my point, dear. How many other children your age could plan something as daring as this?"

"But we aren't going to steal the *Crown Jewels* now, so it's all been a massive waste of time."

"It's not over yet," said Granny, as she pulled out a tin of **cabbage** soup from her handbag. "We can always try some good old-fashioned brute force!"

Granny handed the tin to her grandson. Ben took it with a smile, and then walked over to the cabinet.

"Here goes!" said Ben, as he swung back the tin to strike the glass.

"Please don't," said a voice from the shadows.

Ben and Granny froze in terror.

Was it a ghost?

"Who's there?" Ben called out.

The figure stepped out into the light.

It was *the Queen.*

27

AN AUDIENCE
WITH THE
QUEEN

"What on earth are you doing here?" asked
Ben. "Er… I mean, what on earth are you doing
here, Your Majesty?"

"I like to come here when I can't sleep,"
replied the Queen. She spoke in that instantly
familiar *posh* voice of hers. Ben and Granny were
surprised to see she was wearing a nightgown
and little furry Corgi slippers. She was also
wearing the coronation crown on her head.
It was the most magnificent of all the *Crown
Jewels*. The Archbishop of Canterbury placed
it on her head when she was crowned Queen

in 1953. The crown, which dates back to 1661, is made of gold, encrusted with diamonds, rubies, pearls, emeralds and sapphires.

It was an impressive look, even for the Queen! "I come here to think," the Queen went on. "I got my chauffeur to bring me over from Buckingham Palace in the Bentley. I have my Christmas address to the nation in a few weeks, and I need to think carefully about what I want to say. One always finds it easier to think with one's crown on. The question is, what on earth are you two doing here?"

Ben and Granny looked at each other, ashamed.

Being told off was bad enough at the best of times, but being told off by the Queen was on a whole other level of being-told-offness, as this simple graph demonstrates:

TOLD-OFFNESS

A PARENT · TEACHER · HEAD TEACHER · AIR HOSTESS · LIBRARIAN · POSTMAN · SCOUT MASTER · TRAFFIC WARDEN · PARK KEEPER · VICAR · POLICEMAN · JUDGE · THE QUEEN

"And why do the pair of you smell like poo-poo? Well?" pushed Her Majesty. "I am waiting."

"I am solely to blame, Your Majesty," said Granny, bowing her head.

"No, she's not," said Ben. "It was me who said we should steal the *Crown Jewels*. I talked her into it."

"That's true," said Granny, "but it's not what I meant. I started this whole thing, when I pretended to be an international jewel thief."

"What?" exclaimed Ben.

"Pardon?" said the Queen. "One is terribly confused."

"My grandson hated staying with me on Friday nights," said Granny. "I heard him one night, calling his parents and complaining about how boring I was—"

"But, Granny, I don't think that any more!" protested Ben.

"It's all right, Ben, I know things have changed since then. And in truth I *was* boring. I just liked to eat cabbage and play SCRABBLE, and I knew deep down that you hated those things. So I made up stories from the books I read to entertain you. I told you I was an infamous jewel thief called 'The **BLACK CAT**'..."

"But what about those diamonds you showed me?" said Ben, feeling shocked and angry that he'd been deceived.

"All worthless, dear," replied Granny. "Made of glass. I found them in an old ice-cream tub at the local charity shop."

Ben stared at her. He couldn't believe it. The whole thing, the whole incredible story, was made up.

"I can't believe you lied to me!" he said.

"I-I mean..." said Granny falteringly.

Ben turned to glare at her. "You're not my **gangsta granny** after all," he said.

Then there was a deafening silence in the Jewel House.

Followed by a rather loud and rather posh cough. "Ahem," said an imperious voice.

28

HUNG, DRAWN AND QUARTERED

"I'm terribly sorry to interrupt," said the Queen, in her clipped tones, "but might we get back to the important matter at hand? I still don't understand why the two of you are here in the Tower of London in the middle of the night, smelling of poo-poo, and attempting to steal my jewels."

"Well, once I had started, the lie grew and grew, Your Majesty," continued Granny, avoiding Ben's eyes. "I didn't mean for it to happen. I just got carried away, I suppose. It was so nice to spend that extra time with my

grandson, to have fun with him. It reminded me of when I used to read him bedtime stories. That was in the days when he didn't find me boring."

Ben fidgeted. He was starting to feel guilty too. Granny had lied to him, and that was horrible – but she'd only done it because she was upset that he thought she was dull.

"I had fun too," he whispered.

Granny smiled at him. "I'm glad, little Benny. I'm so sorry, I really —"

"Ahem," interrupted the Queen.

"Oh yes," said Granny. "Well, before I knew it, things had snowballed, and we were planning to take on the most daring robbery of all time. We climbed up the sewage pipe, by the way. We don't usually smell like this, Your Majesty."

"I should hope not.

"PPPPPPPOOOOOOOOOOEEE

EEEEEEEEEEEEEYYYYYYY YYYYYYYYYYYYYY!!!!!!!!!!!!!"

Ben was feeling *really* guilty now. Even if Granny had never been an international jewel thief, she certainly wasn't boring. She had helped plan this robbery with him, and now here they were in the Tower of London at midnight, talking to the Queen!

I have to do something to help her, Ben realised.

"The robbery was my idea, Your Majesty," he said. "I am so sorry."

"Please let my grandson go," interjected Granny. "I don't want his young life ruined. Please, I beg you. We were going to return the *Crown Jewels* tomorrow night. I promise."

"A likely story," murmured the Queen.

"It's true!" exclaimed Ben.

"Please do what you want with me, Your Majesty," continued Granny. "Have me locked up here in the Tower for ever, if you like, but I beg you, let the boy go."

The Queen looked lost in thought.

"I really don't know what to do," said the Queen eventually. "I am touched by your story. As you know, I too am a grandmother, and my grandchildren find me dull sometimes."

"Really?" asked Ben. "But you are the Queen!"

"I know," the Queen chuckled.

Ben was stunned. He had never seen the Queen laugh before. She was usually so serious, and never cracked a smile when giving her speech on TV at Christmas, or opening Parliament, or even watching comedians at the Royal Variety Show.

"But to them I'm just their boring old

granny," she continued. "They forget that I was young once."

"And that they too will be old one day," added Granny, with a meaningful look at Ben.

"Exactly, my dear!" agreed the Queen. "I think the younger generation need to have a bit more time for the elderly."

"I'm sorry, Your Majesty," said Ben. "If I hadn't been so selfish and moaned about old people being boring none of this would have ever happened."

There was an uncomfortable silence.

Granny rummaged in her handbag and offered the Queen a bag of sweets. **"Murray Mint,** Your Majesty?"

"Yes, please," said the Queen. She unwrapped it and popped it into her mouth. "Gosh, I haven't had one of these for years."

"They're my favourite," said Granny.

"And they last so long," added the Queen as she sucked it, before composing herself again.

"Do you know what happened to the last man who attempted to steal the *Crown Jewels?*" enquired the Queen.

"Was he **hung, drawn and quartered?**" asked Ben excitedly.

"Believe it or not he was pardoned," said the Queen with a wry smile.

"Pardoned, Your Majesty?" said Granny.

"In 1671, an Irishman by the name of Colonel Blood tried to steal them, but was caught by guards as he tried to escape. He hid this very crown I am wearing now under his cloak and dropped it on the ground just outside. King Charles II was so amused by Colonel Blood's daring attempt that he set him free."

"I must Google him," said Ben.

"I don't know what Googling is," said Granny.

"Nor me," chuckled the Queen. "So, in royal tradition, that's what I am going to do. Pardon you both."

"Oh, thank you, Your Majesty," said Granny, kissing her hand.

Ben fell to his knees. "Thank you, thank you, thank you so much, Your Majesty…"

"Yes, yes, don't grovel," said the Queen

haughtily. "I cannot abide grovelling. I have met far too many grovellers during my reign."

"I am so sorry, Your Majestical Royal Majesty," said Granny.

"That's exactly what I mean! You're grovelling now!" replied the Queen.

Ben and Granny looked at each other in fear. It was hard not to speak to Her Majesty without grovelling at least a little bit.

"Now jolly along quickly, please," said the Queen, "before this whole place is overrun with guards. And don't forget to watch me on the telly on Christmas Day…"

29

ARMED POLICE

It was dawn by the time they trundled back into **GREY CLOSE**. This time there was no police car to give them a lift. It was a very long way home from London on a mobility scooter. Over the speed bumps they went, bump bump bump, and whirred into Granny's drive.

"What a night!" sighed Ben.

"My word, yes, blimey I do feel rather stiff from sitting on that thing for so long," said Granny, as she eased her old and tired body off the scooter. "I am sorry, you know, Ben," she said after a pause. "I really didn't mean to hurt

267

you. It was just so nice spending time with you, I didn't want it to stop."

Ben smiled. "It's OK," he said. "I understand why you did it. And don't worry. You're still my **gangsta granny!**"

"Thank you," said Granny softly. "Anyway, I think that's quite enough excitement to last a lifetime. I want you to go home, be a good boy, and concentrate on your plumbing…"

"I will, I promise. No more heists for me," chuckled Ben.

Suddenly Granny froze.

She looked up.

Ben could hear a helicopter **WHIRRING** overhead.

"Granny?"

"Shush…!" Granny adjusted her hearing aid and listened intently. "That's more than one helicopter. It sounds like a fleet."

WOOO-WOOO-WOOO-WOOO-WOOO!

The sound of police-car sirens s c r e e c h e d from all around, and within moments heavily armed police surrounded them from every angle. Granny and Ben couldn't see any of the bungalows in the close any more because they were trapped behind a wall of policemen in bulletproof vests. The **WHIRR** of police helicopters overhead was so deafening that Granny had to turn her hearing aid down.

A voice came over a megaphone from one of the helicopters. "You are surrounded. Put down your weapons. I repeat, put down your weapons or we will shoot."

"We haven't got any weapons!" shouted Ben. His voice hadn't broken yet and it came out a bit girly.

"Don't argue with them, Ben. Just put your hands in the air!" shouted Granny over the noise.

The gangsta pair put their hands up. A number of especially brave policemen surged forward, pointing their guns right at Ben and Granny and grabbed hold of them.

"Don't move!" came the voice from the

helicopter. *How can I,* Ben thought, *with a great big policeman holding on to me?*

A flurry of leather-gloved hands made their

way up and down their bodies and fumbled through Granny's handbag, presumably searching for guns. If they had been searching for used tissues they would have been in luck, but they didn't find any weapons.

Ben and Granny were then handcuffed. Out from behind the wall of policemen stepped an old man with a very big nose, wearing a pork-pie hat.

It was Mr Parker.

Granny's nosy neighbour.

#

30

"Thought you could get away with stealing the *Crown Jewels*, did you?" whined Mr Parker. "I know all about your wicked plan. Well, it's over. Officers, take them away. And lock them up and throw away the key!"

The policemen pulled the captives in the direction of two waiting police cars.

"Hang on a sec," shouted Ben. "If we stole the *Crown Jewels*, where are they?"

"Yes, of course! The evidence. All we need to put you two gangstas behind bars for ever. Search the basket of the scooter. At once!" said Mr Parker.

One of the policemen went through the basket. He found a large package wrapped in soggy clingfilm.

"Ah, yes, that must be the jewels," said Mr Parker confidently. "Give it here."

Mr Parker shot Granny and Ben a smug look. He started unwrapping the package.

Quite a few minutes passed until the big package was a little package. Finally, Mr Parker reached the end of the clingfilm.

"Ah, yes, here we are!" he announced, as a tin of cabbage soup fell to the ground.

"Could I have that, please, Mr Parker?" said Granny. "It's my lunch."

"Search her bungalow!" barked Mr Parker.

A few policemen tried to bash open the front door by charging at it with their shoulders. Granny looked on, amused, before venturing, "I've got the key right here, if you'd rather use that!"

One of the policemen approached her and rather sheepishly took the key.

"Thank you, madam," he said politely.

Granny and Ben shared a smile.

He then opened the door, and what seemed like hundreds of policemen charged inside. They frantically searched the bungalow, but after a short while they re-emerged, empty-handed.

"There's no *Crown Jewels* in there, I'm afraid, sir," said one of the policemen. "Just a SCRABBLE set and quite a few more tins of cabbage soup."

Mr Parker's face went red with **FURY.** He had called out half the police officers in the country, all for nothing.

"Now, Mr Parker," said one of the policemen to him. "You are very lucky we aren't arresting you for wasting police time…"

"Wait!" said Mr Parker. "Just because the jewels aren't on them or in the house, doesn't mean they don't have them. I know what I heard. Search… the garden! Yes! Dig it up!"

The policeman put up a calming hand. "Mr Parker, we can't just—"

Suddenly, a light of triumph lit up in Mr Parker's eyes. "Hang on. You haven't asked them where they were this evening. I *know* they went to steal the *Crown Jewels*. And I bet they don't have an alibi for tonight!"

The policeman turned to Ben and Granny, frowning. "Actually, that's not a bad point," he said. "Would you mind telling me where you were tonight?" Mr Parker was positively beaming now.

Just then, another policeman waddled over to them. There was something familiar about him, and when Ben saw his moustache, he knew why.

"Boss, we've just had a call through for you on—" PC Fudge began, holding up a walkie-talkie. He stopped suddenly, staring at Ben and Granny. "Well!" he said. "If it isn't the clingfilm people!"

"PC Pear!" said Ben.

"Fudge!" corrected Fudge.

"Sorry, yes, Fudge. Nice to see you again."

The superior officer looked confused. "Sorry?"

"The lad and his granny. They're the **CLING-FILM APPRECIATION SOCIETY.** They went to their annual meeting in London tonight. I dropped them off, in fact."

"So they weren't stealing the *Crown Jewels?*" asked his boss.

"No!" laughed PC Fudge. "They were merging with the **BUBBLE WRAP SOCIETY.** Stealing the *Crown Jewels* indeed!" He smiled at Ben and Granny. "What an idea!"

Mr Parker had gone red in the face. "But… but… They did it! They're villains, I'm telling you!"

While he was **spluttering,** the superior officer took the walkie-talkie from PC Fudge. "Yep. Uh-huh. Right. Thank you," he said. He turned to Ben and Granny. "That was Special Branch. I asked them to check if the *Crown Jewels* were still there. Turns out they are. I'm sorry, Ma'am. And boy. We'll have those handcuffs off you in a jiffy."

Mr Parker slumped, looking utterly dejected. "No, it can't be—"

"If I hear one more PEEP out of you, Mr Parker," said the policeman, "I will throw you in the cells for the night!" He turned smartly on his heel and walked over to one of the patrol cars, followed by PC Fudge, who waved at Ben and Granny as he left.

Ben and Granny approached Mr Parker, their hands still cuffed together.

"What you heard were just stories," said Ben. "Just my granny telling me stories. Mr Parker, I think you may have let your imagination run away with you."

"But, but, but…!" blustered Mr Parker.

"Me? An international jewel thief?!" Granny chuckled.

The policemen all started chuckling too.

"You'd have to be a bit daft to believe a thing

like that!" she said. "Sorry, Ben," she whispered to her grandson.

"That's OK!" Ben whispered back.

The policemen unlocked the handcuffs, and hastily retreated into their cars and vans and sped off out of **GREY CLOSE.**

"Sorry to disturb you, Madam," said one of the departing officers. "Have a good day."

The helicopters disappeared up into the dawn sky. As the blades got faster, Mr Parker's precious pork-pie hat flew off his head and into a **puddle.**

Granny approached Mr Parker, who was standing hatless in her drive.

"If ever you need to borrow a packet of sugar…" she said kindly.

"Yes…" said Mr Parker.

"Don't knock on my door or I will shove that bag of sugar up your backside," said Granny with a sweet smile.

31

GOLDEN LIGHT

The sun had risen, and **GREY CLOSE** was bathed in golden light. There was dew on the ground, and an unearthly mist made the little row of bungalows look somehow magical.

"Ah well," said Granny with a sigh. "You'd better run home now, young Ben, before your parents wake up."

"They don't care about me," said Ben.

"Oh yes, they do," said Granny, tentatively putting her arm round her grandson. "They just don't know how to show it."

"Maybe."

Ben yawned the biggest yawn he had ever yawned in his life. "Gosh, I'm so tired. Tonight was amazing!"

"It was the most thrilling night of my life, Ben. I wouldn't have missed it for the world," said Granny with a *twinkling* smile. She took a deep breath.

"Oh, the joy of being alive."

Then her eyes filled with tears.

"Are you all right, Granny?" said Ben softly.

Granny hid her face from her grandson. "I'm fine, child, I really am." Her voice wavered with emotion as she spoke.

Suddenly, Ben knew something was very wrong.

"Granny, please, you can tell me."

He held her hand in his. Her skin was soft but worn. Fragile.

"Well…" said Granny hesitantly. "There is one other thing I lied to you about, dear."

Ben had a sinking feeling.

"What's that?" he asked and he squeezed her hand reassuringly.

"Well, the doctor gave me my test results last week, and I told you I was fine. That was a lie. I'm not fine." Granny paused for a moment. "The truth is, I have cancer."

"No, no…" said Ben with tears in his eyes. He had heard about cancer, enough to know it could be deadly serious.

"Just before you ran into him at the hospital the doctor told me the cancer, well, it's very advanced."

"How long have you got left?" spluttered Ben. "Did he say?"

"He said I wouldn't make Christmas."

Ben hugged his granny, as tight as he could, willing his body to share its life force with hers.

Tears were running down his cheeks. It was

so unfair – he'd only really got to know Granny in the last few weeks, and now he was going to lose her.

"I don't want you to die."

Granny looked at Ben for a moment.

"None of us are going to live for ever, my boy. But I hope you never forget me. Your boring old granny!"

"You're not boring at all. You're a proper gangsta! We very nearly stole the *Crown Jewels,* remember!"

Granny chuckled.

"Yes, but not a word of that to anyone, please. You could still get in a whole heap of trouble. It will have to remain our little secret."

"And the Queen's!" said Ben.

"Oh yes! What a nice old dear she was."

"I will never forget you, Granny," said Ben. "You will for ever be in my heart."

"That's the nicest thing anyone has ever said to me," said the old lady.

"I love you so much, Granny."

"I love you too, Ben. But you'd better be running along now."

"I don't want to leave you."

"That's very sweet of you, dear, but if your mummy and daddy wake up and find you gone, they are going to be extremely worried about you."

"They won't."

"Oh, yes, they will. Now, Ben, please be a good boy."

Ben reluctantly rose to his feet. He helped his granny up off the step.

Then he held her close and kissed her on the cheek. He didn't mind her hairy chin. In fact, he loved it.

He loved the whistle of her hearing aid.

He loved that she smelled of **cabbage**. And most of all, he loved that she blew off without even knowing it.

He loved everything about her.

"Goodbye," he said softly.

"Goodbye, Ben."

32

A FAMILY SANDWICH

When he finally arrived home, Ben noticed the little brown car was missing from the drive. It was still very early in the morning.

Where could his parents have gone at this hour?

Nevertheless, he climbed up the drainpipe, through the window, and back into his bedroom.

All that clambering was hard work; he was tired after staying up all night and the wetsuit made him heavier than usual. Ben moved his **PLUMBING WEEKLY**s aside so he could hide the wetsuit under his bed. Then, as quietly as he could, he put on his pyjamas and climbed into bed.

Just as he was about to shut his eyes, he heard the car speed up the drive, and the front door open, and then the sound of his mum and dad sobbing uncontrollably.

"We've looked everywhere for him," said Dad, sniffing. "I don't know what to do."

"It was my own stupid fault," added Mum, through her tears. "We should never have entered him for that dance competition. He must have run away from home…"

"I'll call the police."

"Yes, yes, we must, we should have done that hours ago."

"We have to get the whole country out looking for him… Hello, hello, I need the police, please… It's my son. I can't find my son…"

Ben felt so wretchedly guilty. His parents *did* care about him after all.

Massively.

He leaped out of bed, burst open his bedroom door, and ran down the stairs into their arms. Dad dropped the telephone.

"Oh, my boy! My boy!" said Dad.

He hugged Ben tighter than he had ever hugged him before. Mum put her arms round her son too, until they were one big family sandwich, with Ben as the filling.

"Oh, Ben, thank goodness you came back!" wailed Mum. "Where have you been?"

"With Granny," replied Ben, not quite telling the whole truth. "She's… well, she's very ill," he said sadly. But he could see from his parents' faces that it wasn't a surprise to them.

"Yes…" said his dad uncomfortably. "I'm afraid that she's—"

"I know," said Ben. "I just can't believe you didn't tell me. She's my granny!"

"I know," said Dad. "And she's my mum too. I'm sorry I didn't tell you, son. I didn't want to upset you…"

Suddenly, Ben could see the pain in his dad's eyes. "That's OK, Dad," he said.

"Me and your mum have been up all night looking everywhere for you," added Dad, as he squeezed his son even tighter. "We never would have thought to look for you at your granny's. You always said she was boring."

"Well, she's not. She's the best granny in the world."

Dad smiled. "That's sweet, son. But you could still have told us where you were."

"I'm sorry. After I let you down so badly at the dancing competition, I didn't think you cared about me."

"Care about you?" said Dad, a shocked expression on his face. "We love you!"

"We love you so much, Ben!" added Mum. "You must never think differently. Who cares about a silly dancing competition hosted by TV's Flavio Flavioli? I am so proud of you, whatever you do."

"We both are," said Dad.

They were all crying and smiling now, and it was hard to know if the tears were happy or sad ones. It didn't really matter, they were probably a mixture of both.

"Shall we go to Granny's for a cup of tea?" said Mum.

"Yes," said Ben. "That would be nice."

"And me and your dad have been talking," said Mum, taking her son's hand in hers. "I found the plumbing magazines."

"But—" said Ben.

"It's all right," continued Mum. "You don't have to be embarrassed. If that's your dream, go for it!"

"Really?" said Ben.

"Yes!" chimed in Dad. "We just want you to be happy."

"Only…" continued Mum, "…me and your dad think if the plumbing doesn't work out as a career, it's very important you have something to fall back on…"

"Fall back on?" asked Ben. He really didn't understand his parents at the best of times, let alone now.

"Yes," said Dad. "And we know **ballroom dancing** isn't your thing…"

"No," agreed Ben, relieved.

"So, how do you feel about **ICE DANCING?**" asked Mum.

Ben stared at her.

For a long moment Mum just looked straight back at him, then finally her face cracked and she burst out laughing. And then Dad was laughing too, and even though there were tears still on his face, Ben couldn't help joining in.

33

SILENCE

After that, things were much better between Ben and his parents. His dad even went to the hardware shop with him and bought him some plumbing tools, and they spent an extremely enjoyable afternoon together taking apart a U-bend.

Then, a week before Christmas, the three of them received a late-night phonc call.

A couple of hours later, Ben, Mum and Dad were gathered round Granny's bed. She was in a hospice, which is where people go when the hospital can't treat them any more. She didn't have long left to live. Hours maybe. The nurses said she could go any time.

Ben was sitting anxiously by Granny's bed. Even though she had her eyes closed and didn't seem able to speak, sitting in that room with her was an incredibly intense experience.

Dad paced up and down at the foot of the bed, unsure of what to do or say.

Mum sat looking on, feeling helpless.

Ben simply held Granny's hand.

He didn't want her to slip away into the darkness alone.

They listened to her raspy breathing. It was a horrible sound. But there was only one sound that was worse.

Silence.

That would mean she was gone.

Then, to everyone's surprise, Granny blinked and opened her eyes. She smiled when she saw the three of them. "I'm… famished," she said in a weak voice. She reached under her sheets and took out something wrapped in clingfilm, which she started unpeeling.

"What's that?" asked Ben.

"It's just a slice of cabbage cake," wheezed Granny. "Honestly, the food in here is **ghastly.**"

A little later, Mum and Dad went out to get a coffee from the vending machine. Ben didn't want to leave Granny's side for one second. He reached out and took her hand. It was dry, and so light.

Slowly, Granny turned to look at him. She was running out of time, Ben could see that. She winked. "You'll always be my little Benny," she whispered.

Ben thought how he used to hate that name. Now he loved it. "I know," he said, with a smile. "And you'll always be my **gangsta granny.**"

*

Later, after Granny had finally gone, Ben sat quietly in the back seat of his mum and dad's car as they drove home from the hospice. They were all tired from crying. Meanwhile, loads of people were out Christmas shopping, the roads were full of cars, and there was a long queue outside the cinema. Ben couldn't believe life was going on as normal when something so momentous had just happened.

The car turned a corner and approached the little parade of shops.

"Can I pop into the newsagent, please?" said Ben. "I won't be long."

Dad parked the car, and as a light snow was falling, Ben made his way alone into Raj's shop.

DING! went the bell as the door opened.

"Aah, young Ben!" exclaimed Raj. The newsagent seemed to notice the sad look on

Ben's face. "Is something the matter?"

"Yes, Raj…" spluttered Ben. "My granny just died." Somehow saying that made him start crying again.

Raj rushed out from behind the counter and gave Ben a big hug.

"Oh, Ben, I am so so sorry. I hadn't seen her for a while, and I guessed she wasn't well."

"No. And I just wanted to say, Raj," said Ben between sniffs, "thank you so much for telling me off that time. You were right, she wasn't boring at all. She was amazing."

"I wasn't trying to tell you off, young man. I just thought you had probably never taken the time to get to know your granny."

"You were right. There was so much more to her than I ever imagined." Ben wiped the tears away with his sleeve.

Raj began searching his shop. "Now… I have

a packet of tissues somewhere. Where are they? Oh, yes, just underneath the football stickers. Here you go."

The newsagent opened the packet and passed them to Ben. The boy wiped his eyes.

"Thank you, Raj. Is it ten packets of tissues for the price of nine?" he said with a smile.

"No, no, no!" chuckled Raj.

"Fifteen packets for the price of fourteen?"

Raj put a hand on Ben's shoulder. "You don't understand," he said. "They are on the house."

Ben **stared.** In all the history of the world, Raj had never been known to give anything away for free. It was unheard of. It was madness. It was… it was going to make Ben cry if he wasn't careful. "Thank you so much, Raj," he said quickly, choking up a little. "I'd better get back to my parents. They are waiting outside."

"Yes, yes, but just one moment," said Raj.

"I have a Christmas present somewhere here for you, Ben." He started rummaging around his cluttered little shop again. "Now, where is it?"

Ben's eyes lit up. He loved presents.

"Yes, yes, it's right here behind the Easter eggs. Found it!" exclaimed Raj, as he produced a bag of **Murray Mints.**

Ben was a tiny bit disappointed but he did his best to hide it.

"Wow! Thank you, Raj," said Ben, doing his best school-play acting. "A whole packet of **Murray Mints.**"

"No, just one mint," said Raj, opening the bag, and taking a single **Murray Mint** out before handing it to Ben. "They were your granny's absolute favourite."

"I know," said Ben, with a smile.

34

ZIMMER FRAME

The funeral was on Christmas Eve. Ben had never been to a funeral before. He thought it was bizarre. As the coffin lay at the front of the church, the mourners mumbled their way through unfamiliar hymns, and a vicar who had never met Granny made a tedious speech about her.

It wasn't the vicar's fault, but he could have been waffling on about any old lady who had just died. He went on in a **dreary** monotone about how she liked visiting old churches and was always kind to animals.

Ben wanted to shout out. He wanted to tell everyone, his mum and dad, his uncles and aunts, everyone there about what an incredible granny she was. How she told the most amazing stories.

And most of all he wanted to tell them about the marvellous adventure he had shared with her, how they had nearly stolen the *Crown Jewels* and met the Queen.

But no one would have believed him. He was only eleven. They would assume he had made the whole thing up.

When they arrived home, most of the people who were at the church descended on the house. They drank cup after cup of tea, and ate plate after plate of sandwiches and sausage rolls. It seemed weird having the Christmas decorations up at such a sad time. At first people chatted about Granny, but soon they were gossiping about other things.

Ben sat alone on the sofa, and listened to the adults talking. Granny had left him all her books, and they were now cluttering up his bedroom in great piles. He was tempted to hide away in his room with them.

After a while a kindly-looking old lady moved slowly across the room with her Zimmer frame and eased herself down next to him on the sofa.

"You must be Ben. You don't remember me, do you?" said the old lady.

Ben looked at her for a moment.

She was right.

"Last time I saw you, was your first birthday," she said.

No wonder I don't remember! thought Ben.

"I am Granny's cousin, Edna," she said. "Me

and your granny used to play together as girls, when we were just about your age. I had a fall a few years ago, and I couldn't cope on my own, so I was put into an old folk's home. Your granny was the only person who would come and visit."

"Really? We didn't think she ever went out," said Ben.

"Well, she came to see me once a month. It wasn't easy for her. She had to get four different buses. I was extremely grateful."

"She was a very special lady."

"She was indeed. Incredibly kind and thoughtful. I don't have any children or grandchildren of my own, you see, so me and your granny would sit in the lounge of the old folk's home and play SCRABBLE for hours together."

"SCRABBLE?" said Ben.

"Yes. She told me how much you liked playing it too," said Edna.

Ben couldn't help but smile.

"Yes, I loved it," said Ben.

And to his surprise, he realised he wasn't lying. Looking back, he had loved it. Now his granny was gone, every moment he had spent with her seemed precious. More precious even than the *Crown Jewels.*

"She never stopped talking about you," said Edna. "Your dear old granny said you were the light of her life. She said she would really look forward to you coming to stay on a Friday. It was the best part of her week."

"It was the best part of my week too," said Ben.

"Well, if you like SCRABBLE you must pop over to the old folk's home one day for a game," said Edna. "I need a new partner now your granny's gone."

"That would be great," said Ben.

Later that evening, as his parents watched the **STRICTLY STARS DANCING** Christmas Special, Ben climbed out of his bedroom window and slid down the drainpipe. Without making a sound, he took his bike out of the garage, and cycled to Granny's house one last time.

Snow was falling. It **CRUNCHED** under the wheels of his bike. Ben watched it come down, landing softly on the ground, barely paying attention to his route. He knew the journey off by heart now. He had cycled to the old lady's so many times over the last few months he knew every **bump** and crack in the road.

He stopped his bike outside Granny's little bungalow. There was a scattering of snow on the roof. Post was piled up outside, the lights were all off and there was a "For Sale" sign with icicles hanging off it standing outside.

Even so, Ben was half expecting to see Granny at the window.

Looking at him with that hopeful little smile of hers.

But of course she wasn't there. She was gone for ever.

But she wasn't gone from his heart.

Ben wiped away a tear, took a deep breath, and cycled off home.

He sure had an amazing story to tell his grandchildren one day.

POSTSCRIPT

"Christmas is a special time of year," said the Queen. She was her usual serious self, seated majestically on an antique chair in Buckingham Palace. Once again delivering her annual message to the nation.

Mum, Dad and Ben had just finished their Christmas lunch, and were slumped together on the sofa with mugs of tea watching the Queen on TV, as they did every year.

"A time for families to get together and *celebrate*," Her Majesty went on.

"However, let's not forget the elderly. A few

weeks ago, I met a lady around my age and her grandson, at the Tower of London."

Ben squirmed uncomfortably in his seat.

He glanced at his parents, but they were watching the TV, oblivious.

"It made me think how the young need to show a little more kindness to the elderly. If you are a young person watching this, perhaps give up your seat for an elderly person on the bus. Or help them carry their shopping. Share a game of SCRABBLE with us. Why not bring us a nice bag of **Murray Mints,** once in a while? We old folk do love a nice chomp on a mint. And most of all, young people of this country, I want you to remember this – we old people are certainly not boring. You never know, one day we might even shock you."

Then, with a mischievous grin, the Queen lifted up her skirt to the entire country and flashed her Union Jack knickers.

Mum and Dad spat out their tea all over the carpet in astonishment.

But Ben just smiled.

The Queen's a proper gangsta, he thought. *Just like my granny.*

The End

My Grandmothers

Me with Granny Williams

Me with Granny Ellis and Granny Williams

Me with Arthur and Ivy Williams, my dad's parents

Me with my sister, my mum and her mum, Violet Ellis

David Walliams

THANK-YOUS:

I would like to thank a few people who helped me with this book.

First, the hugely talented Tony Ross for his magical illustrations. Next, Ann-Janine Murtagh, the brilliant head of children's books at HarperCollins. Nick Lake, my hard-working editor and friend. The fantastic designers James Stevens and Elorine Grant, who worked on the cover and text respectively. The meticulous copy editor Lizzie Ryley. Samantha White, for her brilliant work publicising my books. The lovely Tanya Brennand-Roper who produces the audio versions. And of course my very supportive literary agent Paul Stevens at Independent.

Most of all I would like to thank you kids for reading my books. I am genuinely humbled that you come and meet me at signings, write me letters or send me drawings. I really love telling you stories. I do hope I can dream up some more. Keep reading, it's good for you!

Need something
to do while waiting
for your new copy of
PLUMBING WEEKLY?
Read on for AWESOME

GANGSTA GRANNY

ACTIVITIES!

WOULD YOU RATHER...

Which would you rather do? You have to choose one!

Would you rather...

A. Eat Granny's cabbage soup?
B. Eat Granny's cabbage cake?
C. Eat broccoli?

A. Dance the Cha-Cha-Cha?
B. Dance the Macarena?
C. Do the Floss?

A. Go to school on a magic carpet?
B. Go to school on a unicycle?
C. Go to school on a camel?

A. Swim through a sewage pipe?

B. Abseil down the side of a hospital?

C. Drive down a motorway on a mobility scooter?

A. Be attacked by giant slugs?

B. Be attacked by a swarm of killer bees?

C. Be attacked by flesh-eating zombies?

A. Be a supermarket security guard?

B. Be a famous ballroom dancer?

C. Be an international jewel thief?

GANGSTA GIGGLES!

What happened when Gangsta Granny stole a toilet?

The police said there was nothing to go on.

Can you match each outfit with the right name?

GANGSTA GIGGLES!
What do you call Gangsta Granny in a fast-food restaurant?

A hamburglar.

5

6

7

8

E FRUIT COCKTAIL

F EGGS 'N' BACON

G ACCIDENT AND EMERGENCY

H THE UNDERWATER WORLD

ANSWERS: 1e, 2c, 3g, 4d, 5f, 6h, 7b, 8a.

QUIZ

How much do you know about David Walliams' brilliant book? Answer the questions to find out if you're a Groggy, a Gentle or a Gangsta Granny!

1 Which of these is Ben's parents' favourite TV show?

A Dancing on Ice Skates

B So, You Think You Might Be Able to Dance a Little Bit?

C Strictly Stars Dancing

2 How old was Granny when she stole her first diamond ring?

A Seven

B Eleven

C Thirteen

3 Granny's bottom sounds like...

A A duck quacking

B A goose honking

C An owl hooting

GANGSTA GIGGLES!

Why did Gangsta Granny have a shower before the robbery?

She wanted to make a clean getaway.

4 Which of these special offers does Raj the newsagent offer Ben?

A Buy forty-seven packets of Murray Mints, get one free

B Buy six boxes of Rolos for the price of five

C Buy twenty-three Cornettos, get one free

5 Granny is an international jewel thief, who goes by the name of...?

A The Black Cat

B The Purple Panther

C The Lavender Leopard

6 Which of these items is NOT inside Granny's secret biscuit tin?

A Bracelet

B Earrings

C Crown

7 What is the name of Granny's nosy neighbour?

A Mr Meddle

B Mr Snoop

C Mr Parker

QUIZ
(CONT)

8 What are the guards at the Tower of London called?

A Porkmunchers

B Beefeaters

C Chickenchompers

9 When Ben and his granny meet the Queen, what is she wearing on her feet?

A Slippers that look like horses

B Slippers that look like Prince Charles

C Slippers that look like corgis

10 The Crown Jewels have been kept under lock and key in the Tower of London since which year?

A 1903

B 1303

C 1003

SCORES

THREE OR LESS

Oh dear! You're a right Groggy Granny today.
Better wake up from your nap and read the book again!

FOUR TO SEVEN

Not bad! You're a lovely Gentle Granny. Have a cup of tea and read the book again to make sure you know all the answers next time.

EIGHT OR MORE

It's official. You are a Gangsta Granny! No need to read the book again – you know it back to front. And are you sure you're not an international jewel thief in your spare time?

ANSWERS: 1c, 2b, 3a, 4a, 5a, 6c, 7c, 8b, 9c, 10b.

JEWELLERY JUMBLE

Gangsta Granny has collected a LOT of jewellery over the years. Can you unscramble the words to find some of the items she has taken?

WORCN

....

GRIN

....

ACENLECK

....

EGRINRA

....

RATIA

....

ANSWERS: Crown, Ring, Necklace, Earring, Tiara.

TEST YOUR MEMORY

Look at the picture of Granny below for one minute. Then cover with a piece of paper and see how many questions you can answer.

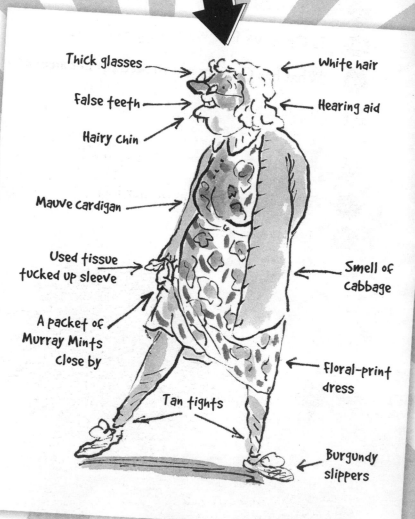

Thick glasses

White hair

False teeth

Hearing aid

Hairy chin

Mauve cardigan

Used tissue tucked up sleeve

Smell of cabbage

A packet of Murray Mints close by

floral-print dress

Tan tights

Burgundy slippers

QUESTIONS:

 1 What colour is Granny's cardigan?

2 What does Granny smell of?

3 Is Granny's hair white or grey?

4 What has Granny got tucked up her sleeve?

   5 What is hairy – Granny's legs or Granny's chin?

6 Is Granny's dress floral or stripey?

7 What is she wearing on her feet?

8 Is Granny wearing a cardigan?

Now check your answers. Give yourself a gangsta high-five if you got more than SIX right!

ANSWERS: 1. Mauve **2.** Cabbage. **3.** White **4.** A used tissue. **5.** Her chin **6.** Floral **7.** Slippers (An extra point if you got burgundy!) **8.** Yes, she is.

HOW TO BLING YOUR GRANNY'S RIDE

IS YOUR GRANNY A GANGSTA? DOES YOUR GRANNY HAVE A MOBILITY SCOOTER THAT NEEDS JAZZING UP? HERE ARE SOME TIPS ON HOW TO MAKE HER SCOOTER A SUPER-DUPER SCOOTER...

Motorbike handlebars

In-basket sound system (plays hymns at 1,000 decibels)

Framed photo of Prince Charles in his swimming trunks

Souped-up lawnmower engine (max speed 12 mph)

GET SOME PLAIN WHITE PAPER AND DRAW YOUR OWN IDEAS!

Retractable knitting needles in wheels (for taking out other scooters in the post-office queue)

HOW TO DRAW
GANGSTA GRANNY!

1) Draw a circle and an interlocking oval like this for Granny's head and body.

2) Add three lines like this for her cardigan and arm.

3) Draw small semicircles across the top of the circle for her hair.

4) Add three curves to wave her hair across her forehead, and three curves beneath for her chin and jawline.

5) Add two small circles for her glasses and draw a hooky line between the circles for her nose. Join the circles to her nose for the bridge over her glasses. Then add her mouth with one semicircle, and a small diagonal line to the right of it.

6) Next draw in two dots for her eyes, add her eyebrows and a line from her glasses to her hair. Draw two triangles beneath her face for her collar. You can ink in the outside curves of her arms now too!

7) Finally, add tone and detail by shading in with your pencil or a little bit of paint or ink, keeping one side more shadowy than the other, to bring your Gangsta Granny to life!